Tempered Journey

Pamela S Thibodeaux

"Your life is a journey you must travel with a deep consciousness of God." ~ 1 Peter 1:18-21 MSG.

Tempered Journey
Book 6 in the Tempered series
by
Pamela S Thibodeaux

Publisher/Distributor:
Temperance Publishing; an imprint of
Pamela S. Thibodeaux Enterprises, LLC
PO Box 324
Iowa, LA 70647

Cover Design: Heaven's Touch Designs

Published in the Unites States of America
Publishing History: First edition November 24, 2023

Dedication

To my faithful Tempered fans who've cried out for Craig to have a follow up story; You who've wondered what happened to Katrina, her children, and Mike Guidry after Scott's death; And for those who wondered what happened to Melena and Garrett from My Heart Weeps.

This Book is for *YOU*

I pray you enjoy Pat Greene's journey into finding true love of her own. And that you are satisfied with the answers to the questions you've posed to me throughout the years regarding the characters you've come to care so much about.

Thank YOU for your continued love and support!

I'd also like to give special *Thanks* to my dear friends, Winona for her aid in developing key scenes in this book, Julia and Janet for their editing expertise, and sweet Delia for the beautiful cover. Without each of you, this book would not have happened so soon.

Chapter One

Pat Greene approached the light of Main St. in Bandera, TX and slapped a palm against her forehead. Tourists crowded the narrow streets. *Should have driven up a couple days earlier to avoid the weekend masses.*

After years of traveling this route, she knew Bandera's population tripled, perhaps even quadrupled, on Hunter's Weekend, which coincided with the Arts & Crafts Fall Fair, in Utopia.

She hadn't factored in that knowledge when planning her trip. And it wouldn't deter her mission to be in Utopia to support her best friend, Melena, since the weekend after the festival, Melena would be getting married.

Six years ago, Melena—a broken widow with no clue as to what God had in store for her after her husband of thirty years passed away—traveled to the Crossed Penn Ranch for an artist's retreat. Afterward, she returned for a summer job. There, Pat's best friend since childhood, had discovered the depths of her artistic ability which catapulted her to a level of success none of them would have imagined. And there, she'd met Garrett Saunders, another illustrious artist known as GS Whitecloud.

Pat sighed, envious of her friend's luck at finding true love twice in her lifetime. Had her call to service—which she will never regret—somehow caused her to miss out on something special?

A flash of movement out of the corner of her eye caught her attention. Pat watched a cowboy, flanked by a younger version of himself, cross the street. Her heart jumped into overdrive. *Dr. Hensley!*

Before she could put her window down and holler, the gentleman, and the boy, climbed into a dark blue SUV, edged out of the Western Store's parking lot, and merged with the traffic moving along at a crawl. She kept the vehicle in view, tempted to follow him. Her phone pinged with a new message.

Are you OK?! We expected you an hour ago.

Pulling onto the shoulder of the road, which would only delay her further, Pat typed her response. *Caught in this ATROCIOUS traffic in Bandera. Should have come with you a week ago.*

But then I wouldn't have seen him.

Pat placed a hand over the thumping in her chest and took a deep breath. Getting her emotions under control, she ended her text with a frustrated-faced emoji followed by a heart and added... *Be there soon.* Sending the message, she eased back onto the road, and inched her way out of town.

The SUV had disappeared from her sight.

She exhaled a long breath, and turned onto the highway leading to Utopia, grateful the number of cars had dwindled. The hilly, winding, roads from Bandera demanded her focus, but didn't stop the memories swarming through her.

Recollections of the one, the only, time they'd been on the same medical mission trip ... The laughter and tears. Joy and sorrow. Tragedies and triumphs...

From all appearances, the man hasn't changed much in thirty years. And boy, was he ever good-looking back then... Deep doe-brown eyes. Thick, dark hair. Strong jaw. Long, muscular frame. Broad shoulders. Handsome *and* the most compassionate heart and generous spirit she'd ever observed in a member of the opposite sex.

The passion they shared.

Almost.

Randy Travis's *On the Other Hand* came on the radio. Pat slammed it off, swallowed hard, and brushed a tear off her cheek. She *had* missed out on something special.

Not because of her career.

Because she'd never met another man who moved her–heart, body, and soul–the way Dr. Richard Scott Hensley had. Less than an hour later, she drove through the Crossed Penn's gate, and her spirits lifted.

Melena always said there's healing energy on this ranch. Being here certainly helped her. Maybe it'll get me out of this funk I've been in for the past year or two or... *Decade.*

Before Pat could disembark from her car, Melena, Garrett, and other members of the ranch staff, filed out of the lodge to gather around her. Pat hugged each of them, and braced herself as Melena flew into her arms with a squeal.

"I'm so glad you made it safe." She pushed back and eyed her with a frown. "Are you OK? You're pale."

Pat barked out a short laugh. "A bit stressed. Guess I'm getting too old to do this kind of traveling. Next time, I'm flying."

Melena pulled her close and whispered, "tell that to someone who doesn't know you so well. We'll talk later." She turned to Garrett. "Get her luggage, please."

Garrett hugged Pat with a chuckle and a wink. "Yes, ma'am. I'll take them to her room while you two catch up."

Melena smiled, and once again, Pat felt a tug of envy. "Thank you."

Pat allowed Melena to hook arms with her, lead her into the lodge, and pour them each a glass of wine. She sipped, grateful no more questions were forthcoming. *For now.* She knew Melena's curiosity, and the love they shared, wouldn't allow her to escape her friend's concern for too long. She listened while Melena chatted on and on about the wedding, and the upcoming fair and art show. "Are the kids coming for the show?"

Melena shook her head. "It's a lot more difficult for them now with their children in school. Well, except for Jon's youngest. Mom is having a ball babysitting when Deborah's mom can't. They'll all be here for the wedding, though." She reached across and grabbed Pat's hand. "I am so glad you came."

Pat closed her fingers around Melena's in a tight squeeze. "Wouldn't miss this for the world."

Garrett strolled toward them with the wine bottle and an extra glass. "Mind if I join you ladies?"

"Of course not." Pat answered, nodding when he offered to top off her drink.

Conversation between the friends never ceased while artists and staff came and went, getting ready for their biggest weekend of the year. After dinner, the hayride, and drinks around the fire, Garrett stood and held out a hand to Melena. "I know you two have a lot more visiting to do, so I'm going to head out. I'll see you both in the morning."

Pat rose, not ready to face the questions she knew Melena would ask. "You don't have to stay with me, Mel."

Melena eyed her, a curious lift to her brow. "You don't want me to spend the night with you?"

Pat's cheeks heated. "No... I mean... Of course, I want you to. I just don't want you to feel obligated."

"Since when has spending quality time together been an obligation?"

Pat closed her eyes and inhaled a deep, cleansing breath. "You know what I mean, Melena."

"Garrett and I see each other all the time. But I will give you your space if that's what you need. I know you had a long journey. I'm sure you're tired."

Pat heard the hurt underlying her tone and felt a tug of remorse. *Since when has sharing your heart with your best friend been a problem?* Never. She touched Melena's cheek. "You're right. I am tired. But I want you to stay. Please do."

Melena walked with Garrett to his truck. Pat watched their tender embrace and fought back the tears of grief, guilt, and envy she'd kept at bay all day. Had she wasted her life waiting, *wishing*, for a feeling she might never find again? Had she passed up the opportunities she'd been given to have a man in her life who would love, honor, and cherish her the way Jon, and now Garrett, did Melena? Was it too late?

Not wanting her friend to see how distraught she really was, Pat headed to the lodge. She climbed the stairs to her room, and slipped into the shower, determined to have her turmoil under control by the time Melena joined her.

Chapter Two

The anguish on her friend's face, as Pat strode toward the lodge, struck like a knife in Melena's chest. "I'm worried about her."

Garrett skimmed his lips across her forehead. "I get the feeling something's off too. I'm sure you will help her sort it all out. Just don't push too much, too soon."

"I won't." She arched an eyebrow at him. "Wait. You think I'm pushy?"

Darkness prevented her from seeing the dimple that danced in his cheek when he smiled, but his chuckle reverberated through her. "I didn't say that."

"But do you?"

"We all have the tendency to be insistent, when those we love are hurting, and always with the best intentions."

He hushed further comments with his mouth. Melena melted against him. "Don't think you can brush me off with a kiss, buddy. This conversation isn't over."

He chortled. "It is for now. Have a good night. See you in the morning."

She waited until he'd turned his truck around, and headed down the drive, before going to Pat's room. She knocked. Waited.

Pat opened the door. "Hey. Look, I'm..."

Melena stopped the apology with a finger against Pat's mouth. "You don't have to apologize to me. Just come here."

A lifetime of love and friendship held them together in an embrace until Pat pulled away.

"I don't know what's going on, but I'm worried about you. You know I'm here if and when you want to talk."

Pat nodded.

"Ok. You ready for bed? Another glass of wine? A movie?"

"How about ice cream and a movie in our pj's."

Melena grinned. "I'll run down and get us some. Be back in a few."

"I'll see if I can find anything interesting on T.V."

Melena hurried down to the kitchen, scooped two huge bowls of milk chocolate decadence laced with dark chocolate chunks, marshmallows, and nuts, then ran back upstairs. Hands full, she knocked with the toe of her boot. The door opened with a swoosh against the carpet. She handed Pat her ice cream. Putting hers on the nightstand, Melena took a moment to change, and wash her face, before climbing on the bed next to Pat's to indulge. "What did you find to watch?" she asked between mouthfuls of gooey goodness.

"A romcom."

Melena stared at her in disbelief. "Really?"

"Either that or blood, guts, gore, and filth. Besides, that's what the 'mute' button is for."

Laughter burst through her so hard, Melena had to cover her mouth to keep from spitting ice cream all over the bed. Which, in turn, gave Pat the giggles. Before they knew it, both were doubled over with mirth, mimicking the plot, and making up lines, for the actors and actresses in the poorly written and produced program. The antics continued until someone knocked on the adjoining wall.

"Hey, you're having too much fun in there."

"Sorry," Melena yelled, while Pat smothered more laughter behind her hand.

Spent, the two flopped back on their beds. Melena changed the channel to a music station, and turned the volume to where it served as a backdrop. Several minutes passed before either could look at the other without burying their face in a pillow to stifle the laughter threatening to erupt.

Pat got up, grabbed their bowls off the nightstand between the beds, and carried them to the bathroom sink to rinse out. "I haven't laughed like this in forever."

Melena scrambled into a sitting position. "Really? Why's that do you suppose?"

Pat shrugged. Melena could tell by her reflection, Pat struggled to answer. She waited, albeit a bit impatiently, for Pat to finish and get back in bed, hoping her friend would open up to her. *I can't be here for her if she doesn't talk to me.*

"I've been feeling a bit... melancholy lately."

A tear slid down her cheek, but the waves of tension emanating from her stopped Melena from simply crawling beside her and taking Pat into her arms. "Any idea why?"

Pat propped pillows against the headboard and shifted positions until she rested against them. "Lots of reasons. I'm tired, for one. And, wondering if I've wasted my life."

"How can you waste your life doing what you love?"

"Not my life, I guess. But, perhaps, squandered the possibility of love and marriage."

Melena hoped the glow in her heart was reflected in her smile. "It's never too late for that."

Pat blew out a breath. Fidgeted. "That's just it. Growing up, I never thought I'd want that. But now, getting older and facing the rest of my life alone, I'm not so sure."

"So, retire. Quit or take a sabbatical. It's obvious these whispers in your heart are the deeper longings of your soul. Listen to them."

"But what would I do? I've been so busy my entire life, I have no idea what I would do if I weren't working."

"Aren't you the one who's always telling others to stop arguing for their limitations and be open to what God is trying to show them? The possibilities are endless. You could go to more of those meditation retreats you love so much. Or develop your own for that matter. Teach others what you know. You can share your gifts, and help people, without globetrotting three-fourths of the year, in numerous ways. Besides, travel is becoming more and more precarious. I, for one, would love to see you settled somewhere stateside."

Melena reached a hand out to her, glad when Pat placed hers in it. "A very wise and lovely friend gave me some advice a while back that saved my life... If you don't do something different, change the status quo, you're not going to make it through this."

Pat squeezed her hand, released it, and fidgeted again. "Did I ever tell you about Scott Hensley?"

Melena searched her mind. "The name sounds familiar... Wait, he's a doctor you met years ago. You two were very close but he was married. Right?"

Pat nodded. "Technically, yes. And trust me, not many of the married men I've worked with through the years, exhibited the same morals as he. But he was also very unhappy and... Alone. Things had been challenging for quite a while. His best friend's wife had miscarried for the second or third time, and Scott felt so badly for them. But his wife was jealous and hateful. She gave him hell for the time he spent with them. He came on the mission trip to get away from all that negativity, and to regain a measure of peace and clarity in his life. Then, she, and his parents, flew over to meet him near the end of the trip. They were killed on the way home."

"Oh, my God. Yes, I remember now. I recall how distraught you were after that, too."

"To say he was devastated is an understatement. So filled with guilt and anger. Pain and resentment. I did the best I could to console him in the time it took for him to get things lined out to leave. Begged him not to go too soon. Especially knowing the details... A senseless act of violence supposedly by a terrorist group."

"You were in love with him." There was more statement than question in her tone. Melena's heart beat double-time, waiting for Pat's answer.

"Yes. I'd never met a man like him. Nor have I to this day. So... Dynamic. Charismatic. Loyal. Honest. *Genuine*. Even now, there are no words to describe the depth of his character." Pat swiped at the tears rolling down her cheeks and took a breath.

"I saw him today."

Melena bolted off the pillow and straightened her shoulders. "What? Where? Are you sure?"

"In Bandera. Only a glimpse, but I knew it was him in every fiber of my being."

"Did you talk to him?"

"No. He had a young boy with him. Not sure if it was his son or grandson, but the spitting image of Scott. I thought about following them, but you texted, and I was already late getting here. Besides, what would I say to him after all these years? I couldn't just drop into his life out of the blue. What if he remarried? What would his wife say?"

"But what if he's not married right now? Just because he had a child with him, doesn't mean he's still with the boy's mother. Wouldn't it be worth it to find out if he is still the man you found him to be back then?"

Pat shrugged.

"That's why you're second-guessing your life."

Pat nodded. "One of the many reasons."

Melena got up, sat beside her, and pulled Pat into her arms. "I'll support you in whatever you decide. I'm here for you. Personally, I think you should consider doing a little research. You always did enjoy staying a few days in Bandera."

Pat hugged her. "I'll think about it. Thank you. I love you."

"I love you, too." Melena eased back over to her bed. "Whew, I'm tired all of a sudden."

Pat chuckled. "Post sugar crash."

"Probably. And all the excitement of the day. And the days to come."

"You and Garrett have your art pieces ready for the fair and the show?"

"Yes. And you should see some of Missy's work. That girl has flourished since she and Brock moved here."

"They seem happy."

"They are. Very. She had a special glow about her today, didn't she?"

Pat gasped. "She's pregnant?"

"Yes, and they are ecstatic. I wasn't supposed to say

anything, so you can't either. They want to make the announcement themselves. But I am so excited for them."

Pat scooted down and tugged the covers over her. "I won't say a word."

Melena listened as Pat's breathing deepened and said a quick prayer for her friend to find the peace and happiness she, herself, enjoyed.

In the days to follow, there was no time to talk about Scott Hensley or what Pat might do about him. As they did every year, each artist to be showcased at the ranch's Annual Art Show, took turns working the booth at the Arts & Crafts Fall Fair in Utopia, where the town square overflowed with vendors offering handmade crafts, homemade jellies and pies, metal, and wood art. Authors touted their books. Flint knappers offered unique knives and sharpening stones. Sculptors displayed pottery and ceramics. Designers set out purses, jewelry, quilts, crocheted items, hand-crafted wind chimes, and toys.

By Monday, all the artists were gone. The ranch house and cabins were cleaned and prepared for Melena and Garrett's wedding. Photos and memorabilia, from Melena and Garrett's lives, were displayed throughout the facilities. Gifts were collected and stored, in anticipation of the reception.

Melena's children, grandchildren, and parents arrived on Thursday. During one of the group dinners, Missy and Brock told everyone of the upcoming addition to their life, which caused a firestorm of enthusiasm and well wishes.

Perfect fall weather provided a colorful, cool ambiance for the outdoor ceremony. The Penn's outdid themselves in providing food and drinks for the wedding. A plethora of appetizers, salads, side dishes, vegetable and beef Shish Kabobs, seafood, and steak entrée's and a variety of pastries and desserts, graced tables inside and out. Centerpieces containing silk Magnolia flowers sat alongside china, crystal, and silverware. Drink stations were strategically placed around the grounds where people mingled. Chairs were draped in fabric and lace to match and accentuate Melena's dress.

With her granddaughters serving as flower girl and bridesmaid, and oldest grandson as ring bearer, Melena, and Garrett, stood beneath an arbor decorated with flowers native to the area, and pledged to love, honor, and cherish one another. "You've encouraged and challenged me to grow in ways I never dreamed possible–mentally, emotionally, spiritually, even professionally. I will do the same for you, even if that means spending time apart," she vowed.

The absolute love, and joy, on Garret's face, at hearing her youngest grandson insist, rather loudly, to, "go meet G'mpa Gawet," would be etched in her mind forever. Melena promised herself to transfer his expression onto canvas as soon as humanly possible.

Her heart overflowed when Garrett cupped her face in his hands and declared, "I'll never interfere with your memories of Jon and will respect the times you still feel the need to grieve him. But, I will gladly spend the rest of my life having adventures and treasuring new memories with you."

Laughter twittered throughout the assembly, when he kissed his bride, long before the Justice of the Peace gave him permission. Hand-in-hand, they turned to face their family and friends, and found not a dry eye in the crowd.

Later, Melena removed the bolero, and turned for her daughter to unzip the pale pink crepe dress garnished with embroidered Magnolias. The rich green leaves of Mississippi's state flower matched her eyes.

"This ensemble is absolutely gorgeous, Mom. Wherever did you find it?"

"At a little boutique off the beaten path somewhere in Georgia." She hung the outfit in a garment bag for her daughter to take home and changed into comfortable jeans and a sweater. She and Garrett were about to embark on what they'd laughingly called a "working" honeymoon in Europe's most romantic places. Venice, Paris, and Athens.

One by one, her family members filed out, leaving her, and Pat, totally alone for the first time in a week. Pat sniffed back tears and held her close. "I'm elated for you, Mel. Now go and live your happy-ever-after."

Melena hugged her tightly, knowing her voice reflected the nostalgia in her heart. "Which we both know is a fairytale. Real life throws challenges at you that can blow 'happy ever after' to smithereens. But I am grateful for the love God has blessed me with. And another opportunity to give said fairytale a go. You've spent a lifetime in service to others, Pat. *You* deserve to be happy too. There's a reason this man showed up, now, when you're questioning everything. Promise me you won't miss out on the chance to discover why. Take a gamble on finding your own bliss."

"I promise."

"Good. I'll be checking in to see that you do. And I

expect a report as soon as you find him."

Pat snickered. "Yes, ma'am."

The two of them went downstairs. Melena joined her husband and family for one last round of goodbyes, then the newlyweds drove away.

Chapter Three

Craig Harris poured a drink then set the whiskey bottle on the porch rail. Settling in his chair, he leaned back, sipped, and closed his eyes. He'd need earplugs to shut out the sounds of disorder that occurred every night when his son, and daughter-in-law, put their children to bed. Particularly after a weekend filled with familial fun and laughter.

Beginning with the football game on Friday night, the Harris/Hensley clan had spent the last few days enjoying the cooler air fall brought to Bandera.

Two years ago, they moved his brother's widow, and their kids, from Lafayette, Louisiana, into the house he'd built between his ranch and Scott's childhood home, now known as the Hensley House B&B. They ditched their original thoughts of dismantling the business, when the profit and loss statements came in from the accountant the January following Scott's death. Craig immediately signed the proceeds over to Katrina, who'd adamantly refused to accept them. Knowing she, and the kids, would be moving when the school year ended, he sank the money into a house for them. He then had his lawyer draw up papers that put further profits from the business into trusts for his niece and nephews.

Mike Guidry, Scott's longtime friend and colleague, soon followed. He now resided in the studio apartment of the Hensley House and enjoyed a flourishing medical practice. As Scott had years ago, Mike was one of the few doctors who made house calls. That there were mutual feelings between him, and Trina came as no surprise. Even Scott had foreseen a possible relationship between the two.

A soul-deep ache pierced his heart. Craig swallowed the last sip of his drink, and the surge of grief clogging his throat. Per their nightly custom, his son walked out of the house to join him. Ace filled Craig's glass then poured one for himself.

"How's it going, Dad?"

Craig tipped the rim against his mouth, took a drink. "It's goin'. Y'all finally get them settled down?"

Ace downed his shot in one gulp, exhaled on a hiss, and poured another. "Yep. Parenting isn't the easiest job in the world."

"No. But it's worth every moment of madness."

Ace grinned. "Easy for you to say. You get to hang around and spoil them. We have to do all the disciplining."

Craig chortled. "Grandfather's prerogative."

Ace's sigh echoed in the still night air. They rocked in companionable silence for a few minutes. "Hard to believe another year has almost come and gone."

"You know what they say... Time flies when you're having fun."

"Are we?"

"Are we what?"

"Having fun yet."

Ace's grin, and expression, reminded him of his wife so much that Craig couldn't answer. He simply arched an eyebrow in response.

Ace laughed. "More like barely controlled chaos if you ask me."

Craig nodded, attempting a smile. "True."

Ace leaned toward him. "What's wrong, Daddy? You

seem a bit down in the mouth lately.”

Craig cleared the lump from his throat. “Missing Mama, Ace.”

“That never really goes away. Does it?”

Craig shook his head, and blinked hard, but refrained from commenting.

“It’s more than that, though. Isn’t it?”

Craig lifted one shoulder in answer.

Ace rolled out of his chair and squatted beside Craig’s. “You know, Scott asked me a long time ago, how I would feel if you found another wife. Back then, I couldn’t even fathom it. But life goes on, Daddy, and it’s too short, or maybe too long, to live it alone. Mama wouldn’t want you to. Nor would she want you to still be grieving this much.

“You should go out once in a while. Find a companion, or even marry again. None of us would begrudge you that. I mean, look at Trina and Mike. They’re not rushing into anything, but you can tell by observing them, they’re a couple. They have each other, as well as their own space. It’s OK for you to have that, too. If you want it.”

Craig tugged his son close for a brief hug and pressed his lips against the silky blond hair Ace had inherited from his mother. “Thanks. I’ll keep that in mind.”

Ace gave him a quick squeeze and rose. “I’m going inside. The kids are waiting for goodnight hugs and kisses from their PaPaw.”

Craig chuckled. Nothing brightened his life more than the unrestrained affection of his grandchildren. “I’ll be in shortly to oblige them.”

“Oh, while I’m thinking about it, we need to pick up

that load of feed I ordered. I've got a full day at the vet clinic tomorrow, so...?"

"I'll go into town and get it."

Ace acknowledged his remark, with a slight incline of his chin, then went in the house.

Craig sat alone a few minutes longer, then followed.

The next morning, he awakened to the same bedlam as the night before.

Kids whining.

Adults fussing.

Named after her grandmother, Tamera Joy didn't want to go to school. Little Ace cried because his sister was upset.

Craig exited his room as she stomped her foot and reiterated her demand to stay home. Maybe she should be nicknamed Temper also, he thought with a smile, but didn't dare voice that aloud.

Ace hissed in a breath, told his son to sit still, and squared off with her. Her eyes widened when he squatted eye-level with her and clasped her chin in a firm hand. "Tamera Joy, if you don't straighten up right now, I'm going to paddle your behind, and you'll be grounded for the week."

She started to argue when she spotted him. A smile lit her face. "PaPaw!"

At his son's imploring glance, Craig stopped his granddaughter from running toward him. "Good morning, sweetheart. Finish your talk with Daddy and then you can come give me a hug."

"Thank you," Ace mouthed.

Craig nodded, smiled.

Tamera Joy gazed at her father with pleading eyes

and trembling lip. "I'm sorry, Daddy. But I really don't want to go to school today."

"I know you don't. I don't want to go to work, either. But sometimes we have to do something whether we want to or not. Do you understand?"

She nodded. "Yes, sir."

"Good. Now give PaPaw a hug, and let's go."

Craig welcomed the embrace, and smothered her with kisses, until little girl giggles filled the air. "Where's Lex?" he asked when she stood beside her father once more.

Ace ran a hand through his hair. "Sick."

At three months along, she wasn't sailing through this pregnancy as she had the first two. "I'll keep Little Ace with me today."

"Thanks, Dad." Ace's tone reflected relief, but the fact her baby brother was spending the day with her PaPaw only inflamed Tamera Joy once more.

"That's not fair, I want to go with PaPaw too!"

Craig watched his son struggle for patience and stepped toward them. "How about we pick you up after school, and we'll go to the park. *If* that's OK with your parents."

"Can we, Daddy? Can we?"

Ace shook his head but warded off her wails with a firm grip on her arm. "You think you deserve to go to the park with the way you've behaved this morning?"

Again, tears clouded the beloved green gaze. A frown carved a cavern in her face. "No, sir."

She sniffled, breaking both men's hearts.

"Well, at least you know when you're wrong. I'll let you go. This time. But Tamera Joy, if you ever, and I mean, *ever,* act this way again you *will* be grounded. Do. You. Hear. Me?"

Brighter than the sun on a summer day, her smile melted the anger out of the air as its counterpart would snow. She threw herself into her father's arms, kissed his cheek, and solemnly thanked him.

Craig held his grandchildren's hands, and the three made their way down the stairs while Ace checked on his wife.

Once his son and granddaughter were on their way, Craig settled his grandson in his booster seat, at the table, and handed him a cup of juice. Knowing the boy wouldn't sit still for long, he prepared a tray with dry toast, and tea, and carried it to his daughter-in-law. "I'm taking the baby and heading to Amber's for a while."

Lexie's smile wavered. "Thanks."

Craig hesitated. "Would you prefer if I stay here? You're awfully pale."

She moaned, placed a wet cloth across her mouth, and shook her head. After several deep breaths she said, "I'll be fine."

"OK. Call if you need anything. I can be back in a jiffy."

Her smile didn't waver as much this time. A sure sign the nausea was passing. "Trina said the same thing."

Gathering a diaper bag, he returned downstairs, bundled Little Ace into his jacket and hat, and headed to his daughter's house.

Amber took the boy in her arms, accepted his excited, "bamber, bamber!" and big, smacking kiss with a laugh. "How's Lexie?"

"Having a rough morning. That's why I've got the

baby."

"Not for long," Stanley quipped, and held his arms out for Little Ace to climb into for his share of hugs and kisses. When he headed outside to work with a colt he had to deliver to the new owner over the weekend, the child followed on wobbly legs.

"Watch him close." Craig smirked at the admonishing glare from his son-in-law.

Amber wiped a tear off her cheek, and watched out the kitchen window, as the two made their way to the corral. "I know it's crazy to feel so bereft. We have three beautiful children. But..."

Craig hugged his daughter, understanding all-to-well their grief after miscarrying for the second time, and finding they could not have more children. "It's not crazy. It's normal. And yes, you have three beautiful, healthy kids. A niece and nephew. Another on the way. And a slew of cousins. There's no lack of youngsters around here for you to love and spoil."

He rolled his eyes for emphasis. She laughed—as he hoped she would—and hugged him.

"Thank you, Daddy. Would you like a cup of coffee?"

"I'd love one."

The hours rolled by. Stanley brought Little Ace in for his midmorning snack and nap. He joined them a while later for lunch, over which he announced he needed to head into town for horse wormer.

Craig tapped the tabletop with a fist. "Damn. Forgot. I'm supposed to pick up feed today. And I promised Tamera a trip to the park after school."

"I can get the feed for you."

"I've got a better idea," Amber inserted. "Why don't

we," she wagged a finger between her and Stanley. "Pick up Tamera, get our girls and William, and take them all to the park. You can get your load of feed and Stan's supplies."

"You sure you don't mind?"

Amber shook her head. "We'd be delighted. Might call Trina and have her meet us there with her brood. We'll grab dinner for everyone—I'm sure Lexie does not feel like cooking—and you can have an afternoon and evening to yourself. You look like you need one."

The smile she bestowed on him took the sting out of the words. Craig chuckled. "You know me too well."

"Of course, I do." Amber rose from her chair, wrapped her arms around him, pressed a kiss, and then rested her cheek against his head. 'You're my first love. My hero."

Craig sent his son-in-law a smug look.

Stanley scraped back from the table with a sneer. "Yeah, but I'm her best."

Craig laughed. He'd enjoy ribbing Stanley, as he had for years, until the day he took his last breath. Before he could respond, they heard the baby's feet hit the floor. He ran in to meet them as fast as his legs could carry his small, chubby body.

"Hey, Buckaroo."

Little Ace put his hands on his hips and glared at Stanley. "I not buk-a-woo. I widdle Ace."

"Don't let Lexie hear you call him that," Craig warned.

Stanley tossed the baby into the air. "We're not afraid of mean, ol' Lexie."

A burst of high-pitched guffaws rang out across the

room.

Craig called Ace, and then Lexie, to fill them in on the change of plans, and went back to the ranch to trade the SUV for his truck and trailer. By the time he retrieved the feed, and the other items Ace, and Stan, needed, he was hot, tired, and hungry.

Nothing a hamburger steak and cold beer won't fix.

He pulled into the parking lot of his favorite diner and climbed out of the truck. Making sure the trailer gate and cover were securely latched, he donned his hat and went inside.

Craig ate his supper, then enjoyed a piece of coconut pie and a cup of coffee. The cowbell above the door clanged. Standing in line to check out, he glanced over as a slender woman with spiky blond hair stepped through the entrance. Her gaze met his—not the rich sapphire of his wife, daughter, and granddaughters, nor the lighter shade of Stanley's, but the hot blue of a flame. Almost purple.

A sharp, sweet sensation Craig hadn't felt in years, hadn't thought he'd ever feel again, zinged through his system all the way to his toes.

She hesitated, took a step toward him, and paled a degree or two. Those beautiful eyes widened in shock and disbelief. "Dr. Hensley?" She edged closer. "Scott?"

The jagged blow of grief nearly brought him to his knees. Craig shook his head. "No, ma'am. Scott's dead. I'm his brother, Craig."

Chapter Four

Pat's world tilted on its axis. Every ounce of blood drained from her limbs. Her knees threatened to buckle. He grabbed her arm, eased her into a seat, and sat in the chair across from her. "D-d..." She cleared her throat. "Dead? When? How?"

"He died three, almost four years ago now. Emergency room incident."

"Oh, my. I am so sorry." *Could have found that information on the internet and avoided this fiasco.* Except she always felt a web search on someone was an invasion of privacy. "I didn't know he had a brother."

The smile she received from that remark, sent her emotions into a tailspin.

"Neither did he. Until 2001, that is. Before then, we'd been best friends our entire life."

"Craig? Are you the friend whose wife had a miscarriage or two? The one Scott's wife envied and hated."

Craig's frown held more than a hint of confusion.

"I'm sorry. I shouldn't have said that. I thought you knew how she felt."

Craig's eyes narrowed into tiny slits of steel. "How who felt? I'm not following you. You sure you don't have us mixed up with someone else? Scott's wife and I are fine."

Pat's turn to frown. "So, he did remarry. I meant his first wife. The one who was killed along with his parents."

The relief on Craig's face was almost comical. He grinned, and her heart nosedived into her stomach.

"You must have known him a really long time ago,

sweetheart."

Heat scorched her cheeks. "Lifetime ago. Please tell me he found peace and happiness after all he went through back then."

Craig nodded. "He did. Let me buy your dinner, and you can tell me how you know my brother."

Pat glanced out the window at the darkened sky. She'd intended to get her meal to go and eat it in her hotel room. She glanced at her watch. Melena would be calling her in less than an hour. "It's getting late. I don't want to hold you up. But thank you."

His cellphone rang, stopping further conversation. Pat placed her order while he talked with whoever was on the other end of the call. Before she could take care of it herself, he grabbed her bill, and walked to the counter. Tucking the phone between his ear and shoulder, he signed the ticket, ended his conversation, snapped the phone shut, and walked out with her.

"Where are you staying?"

She eyed him, a curious lift to her brow.

"I'll follow to make sure you get there safely. Wouldn't want anything to happen to an old friend of Scott's."

Pat pointed in the direction she was heading. "At the hotel right around the corner."

Once again, his smile did funny things to her insides. He gestured for her to lead the way, held his hand out for her keys, and opened the car door for her.

"You gonna be in town a while, or do you live here now?"

"Planned on being here a few days."

"Hope to see you again."

"I'd like that." She'd buckled her seatbelt before she realized she didn't even know his last name. Acting on impulse, Pat rolled her window down and waved him back over. "Hey. How can I reach you?"

The streetlight in the diner's parking lot shone on his mouth, turned up at the corners, and eyes dancing like dew drops off sheet metal. "Check your receipt."

He followed her to the motel and watched until she was safely ensconced in her room. Pat waved, closed the door, and peeked through the curtains as he drove away. She'd barely finished her meal when her cellphone rang. Melena's name and picture flashed on the screen. "Hey, Mel. How's Venice?"

They'd arrived in Rome two days after the wedding, stayed a few days, then took the train to their next destination.

"Oh, it's beautiful, Pat. Garrett, and I have, a ton of pictures already. The ride was amazing in itself. How are you?"

"I'm fine. What time is it over there?"

"It's oh... One-thirty."

"In the morning? Goodness! Have y'all had any sleep at all?"

"Yeah. We took a nap once we got to our hotel. Out enjoying a bit of the nightlife."

"Talk to your kids? Everyone OK?"

"I talked to both before calling you. Are you still at the ranch?"

"No. I'm in Bandera."

"Good. And?"

Pat toed off her boots and leaned back on the bed. "And I ran into his brother today. I didn't even know he had a brother."

"So, did you ask him about Scott?"

A wave of sorrow stole her breath. Pat closed her eyes and struggled to get the words past her tight throat. "He's dead, Mel. Passed away nearly three years ago."

"Oh no! Oh, Pat. I'm so sorry. Are you OK?"

"Kinda numb, but yeah. I mean, I hadn't seen him in decades, but it still came as a shock."

"I'm sure. Did his brother say what happened?"

"All he said was an ER incident."

"So, what are you going to do now?"

Pat took the receipt out of her pocket—which wasn't a receipt but register tape with a phone number scribbled on it—and couldn't help but smile. "I'm going to stay here, for a few days, and talk with his brother."

"Do I sense a hint of interest there?"

Pat held the slip of paper against the giddy rhythm of her heart and laughed. "I swear, Mel, they could pass for twins. Except Craig—that's his name—has gray eyes, where Scott's were brown. From what I can remember, everything else about them is identical. Same height and build. An air of confidence that borders on cockiness. Same sense of humor. That cowboy charm."

"You gained all that from just one meeting?"

"Weird, huh?"

The joy in Melena's voice could not be mistaken. "I think it's wonderful. Keep me posted."

Pat promised and disconnected the call. She'd showered, changed into pajamas, and snuggled back in bed, before the full impact of the joy, shock, grief, and excitement she experienced in the span of an hour, assaulted her system. Tears poured down her cheeks.

Sobs ripped through her in painful torrents.

The following morning, she bundled into her robe and drifted down to the hotel lobby for a cup of coffee. The registration clerk eyed her with more than a hint of concern.

"Are you OK?"

Pat hadn't even bothered to comb her hair or wash her face, so she knew she must look a fright. She smiled. "Rough night. But I'm fine. Thanks for asking."

"Beautiful morning. The sunrise is always magnificent this time of day. There's a really great view from the swimming area."

Pat thanked the young woman and carried the large coffee with her to the suggested vista as the sun peeked over the horizon. Fingers of pink and peach, then yellow and orange, reached down to bathe the hills in splendid hues. Darkness bled from the sky and gave way to the beauty of another day. *Think I'll go for a hike.*

That decided, Pat went back into her room, and dressed in faded jeans, a gray-plaid flannel shirt, and denim jacket. She drove to the Hill Country State Natural Area. There, in a glorious protrusion of rock reaching for the sky among fields of fall flowers, and the colorful foliage of the trees, she found the peace to make a decision.

She'd take a page out of Melena's book and quit her job, or at least take a sabbatical, and see what God had to offer for this next chapter in her life.

She spent the rest of the day sending emails and faxes to her employers, arranging an extended leave of absence. The next afternoon, when Melena called, she informed her friend of her decision and accepted

Garrett's gracious offer to stay in his cabin for as long as she needed. She checked out of the hotel, drove to the Crossed Penn ranch, and retrieved his spare key from Anne, and settled in.

In a spur-of-the moment decision, she went back into Bandera, for dinner and dancing, at a local establishment that provided cooking pits, and sides, for their weekly "steak night."

Chapter Five

Craig awoke groggy and heavy-headed. For the past two nights, dreams and visions disturbed his sleep. Memories of the love and passion he, and Tamera, shared were swallowed by a big, black hole of despair. Then, a spark of light and images of a woman who touched his soul in a way he never thought possible again.

What was he thinking giving her his number?

What if she didn't call?

What if she did?

Round and round, the questions rolled, inciting a host of emotions that left him as empty as a hollowed log. Throwing back the covers, he stumbled into the bathroom, turned the water on as hot as he could stand, and stepped beneath the pulsating spray. *Thank God for hot water and good water pressure.*

Considering the number of people in the house, and the constant influx of those coming and going, the water heaters he'd changed out less than a year ago had been a godsend. *There'll soon be one more.*

Craig winced at the thought. As much as he loved his children and grandchildren, he sometimes wished for a place to simply sit in peace and quiet. A picture of his old hunting cabin flashed through his head. He hadn't been there in years. Wonder what it would take to clean it up? Make it livable.

Didn't matter. He knew as soon as the thoughts crossed his mind, repairing, remodeling, or replacing the old place had just topped his 'to do' list.

Standing in front of the bathroom sink, he wiped the

fog from the mirror, and took a long look at the man staring back at him. Pain and loss had undoubtedly taken their toll. Gone was the sparkle that usually lit his gaze. His cheeks were sunken. Deep lines furrowed the skin around his eyes and mouth. Mirrors might not always tell the whole truth, but this one showed how far down in the pit he'd been.

At that moment, Craig admitted what he'd done his best to hide from himself and his children… The loneliness eating away at his soul.

Had his loyalty to Tamera's memory closed off his heart?

Craig.

He heard her voice as clearly as if she were standing beside him. Tamera… *Temper?*

Life's too short, or perhaps too long, to live it alone.

His son's words but her voice.

It's time. Past time for you to find love. To be happy. Do it for me.

He clenched a fist to keep from putting it through the thin glass covering the medicine chest and let the tears come. Huge, heaving sobs wracked his entire frame. Spent, he removed the cross necklace she'd given him on their wedding day. He traced the beloved engraving with his thumb. *Always, Tamera.*

He blinked back another deluge. Swallowed another lump. Taking the ring off his finger, he added it to the chain, and refastened the clasp.

Would any woman find him attractive? Would he find another who loved him for himself, and not for what he has, as Tamera had?

Again, the image of short, spiky blonde hair and

indigo eyes rose in his mind. His body responded with a flare of desire so sharp it was almost painful. Craig wrapped the towel around his waist and went into the bedroom to dress. Donning his oldest shirt, ragged jeans, battered work hat, and ancient boots, he went downstairs to meet the day.

"Hey, Dad."

Craig acknowledged his son's greeting with a nod. "Ace."

"What's on your agenda for the day?"

Craig poured a thermos of coffee. "Going out to the old hunting cabin. See what kind of shape it's in."

"Want some company?"

He eyed Ace and, for the first time in a long time, decided to be completely honest with his son. "Not really. I'd rather be alone today. But thanks for the offer."

A moment of shock followed by understanding lit Ace's face. His gaze traveled to Craig's left hand, then back up to meet his, eyebrow arched in question. Craig withdrew the chain from around his neck for his son to see. "Didn't want to take a chance on ripping off a finger. No telling what kind of shape the old cabin is in or how much work it'll take to get it back in decent condition."

Ace bit back a smile but couldn't hide the glint in his eyes. "Smart. You might consider taking that off also. Wouldn't want you to break it and lose something."

Craig nodded in agreement but didn't move to do so. *Not yet.* He prepared himself lunch, a jug of tea, and, kissing his grandchildren goodbye, left the house.

* * *

Ace took the stairs two at a time and burst through the bedroom door as Lexie exited the bathroom. "He took off his ring!"

"What?"

"Yeah. And he's going out to the old hunting cabin to see what it'll take to 'get it in decent condition.'" He finger-quoted the words.

"You think he's met someone?"

"I don't know but I think he's opening to the possibility. I've got to tell Amber." He unsnapped the cellphone from its holster.

"Don't you think you ought to wait and not get her hopes up? You know how she worries about him."

Ace's excitement dimmed at the thought of how sensitive his sister was regarding their father. "You're right. Hey, how about steak night, tonight?"

Lexie laughed. "Wanna help him along, do you?"

Heat climbed into his cheeks. "That obvious, huh?"

She hugged him. "Yeah, and I love you for it. Steak night sounds wonderful. Call Amber and I'll call Trina. Let's do this."

* * *

Craig arrived home later that day to find everyone dressed and ready to leave. "What's going on?"

Lexie tugged Little Ace's sweater over his head, bent to kiss him, and then smiled at Craig. "Heading to steak night. We've got one for you, so meet us there."

Craig heaved a tired sigh and wiped his forehead on his arm. *Whew.* "Think I'll grab a sandwich and call it a night."

"You can't. Everyone is coming. It won't be a family dinner if you're not there."

He huffed out a breath. "Ok. I'll see y'all in a bit."

Lexie gathered the baby into her arms and kissed Craig's cheek on her way out the door.

Craig climbed the stairs and stood a long time in the shower. Every muscle in his body ached. The last thing he felt like doing, was getting dressed again, and heading into town. Why hadn't he stood his ground when he told Lexie he wanted to stay home?

Never have time for myself.

The thought screamed through him, adding another layer of guilt to the thick film already coating his mind.

Guilt because he knew they worried about him. Guilt for wanting, needing, space from those he loved. Guilt because he'd spent the whole day thinking about a woman other than the one he'd lost more than a decade ago. Her voice rose in his mind again, urging him to get on with his life. *I'm trying, Temper...*

He considered putting the ring back on his finger but decided against it. No sense in having to take it off again in the morning.

He dressed, grabbed his wallet, keys, and phone, and took off before he changed his mind. His phone signaled a message before he got out of the ranch drive. Ace wanted to know his ETA. Craig messaged back and continued on his way.

He parked his truck and made his way toward the busy entrance. The hostess waved him through, saying his cover charge had already been paid. Craig thanked her, went to the bar, bought himself a beer, got his food, and joined his family. Stanley brought the steaks fresh off the pit before he could settle in.

The adults took turns watching the kids while others danced. As the evening wore on, Craig mingled through the crowd, shaking hands, and visiting with people he hadn't seen in a while.

On his way back to the table he saw her. Sitting alone on a stool by the railing that separated the dance floor from the eating area.

She smiled.

He tipped his hat and tried not to stare. Should he ask her to dance? Invite her over? What would his children say? In all the years they'd come here for steak night, he'd yet to dance with anyone other than his family. Did they notice the way his gaze bounced back to her of its own volition? Why in the hell did he, a man on the backside of sixty, feel like an awkward teenager?

Amber confirmed his fears when she leaned toward him and whispered, "ask her to dance."

"Who?" He tried to feign nonchalance, but his daughter knew him too well.

"That lady over there. She keeps looking over here, and you keep looking back. Do you know her?"

"Amber…" Stanley's tone held warning which she halted with one glare.

"I'm just asking."

Craig downed the remainder of his beer. What was he supposed to say? He didn't even know her name. "Not really. Ran into her at Harry's old place the other night."

"Well, ask her to dance."

Someone beat him to the asking before he could move in her direction. Craig's relief was short-lived when she politely declined the other man's offer. "I'm getting another beer. Anybody want something while I'm going?"

His question was met with a round of no-thank-you, and a flurry of activity, as everyone suddenly wanted to leave. Which quelled his notions of buying himself, much less her, a drink. *Please don't let her leave before I get a chance to talk to her.*

Chapter Six

Pat noticed Craig's family gather their children and prepare to leave. Jackets. Hats. Grumbles and whines. She'd watched the boisterous group all evening. Sons? Grandsons? She didn't know, but she had no doubt some of those boys were his. Or Scott's. She loved seeing Craig dance with the ladies at his table. *The man can move.* In fact, every man at that table had dance moves as smooth as silk.

She'd done her fair share of dancing that night too. She'd arrived at the dancehall and found the Crossed Penn crew had the same idea as her. They, and a couple of artists-in-residence, had settled at a long table and insisted she join them. They'd laughed and joked and two-stepped until, one by one, everyone departed.

She switched seats to get a closer look at Craig and his bunch. *Should I go over and say hello?* she wondered when he tipped his hat in recognition. Within moments of making eye contact, his family headed out. He walked with them to the entrance, hugged everyone, then turned and strode toward her. *Oh, my. Now,* that's *a cowboy if I've ever seen one. With a capital C.*

"Buy you a drink?"

"Sure. Thanks."

He went to the bar and returned with a beer for himself and a wine cooler for her.

"You... uh..." He took a swig. "Lose your receipt?"

She laughed. "No."

"You haven't used it."

Another laugh. "I was raised to let the guy do the pursuing."

He grinned, took another sip, and asked her to dance. Pat gave him her hand, surprised at the sparks shooting up her arm when he twirled her onto the floor for a fast two-step. Pleased at how easily they fell into stride together. The song ended. He escorted her back to the table. Tiny shivers ran along her spine from where his hand rested on her back.

He touched his bottle to hers. "I understand, and appreciate, the way your parents raised you. But kinda hard to be the one to pursue, when this guy doesn't even know your name."

She couldn't stop the giggles when he joined in with a hearty laugh of his own. Swallowing another bout of mirth, she held out her hand for him to shake. "Pat Greene. With an 'e'."

He raised her knuckles to his mouth. "Nice to meet you."

The band started winding down. Craig walked with her to her car.

"How about lunch tomorrow?"

"That would be lovely. Where should I meet you?"

"I can pick you up at the hotel."

She shook her head. "I checked out this morning. I'm staying at a friend's cabin in Utopia."

"I see. OK, then. How about the same diner where we met the other night. Say, eleven or one? Skip the noon rush."

"One o'clock it is."

His smile took her breath away. "See you then."

* * *

Pat awoke filled with a sense of excitement and adventure. She completed her daily ritual of breathing exercises, yoga, and journaling. Preparing a fruit smoothie, she sat at the table and reminisced about last night... The strength of Craig's arms... The way their bodies fit together, moving in perfect rhythm while dancing. The heady attraction and ... *comfort* she felt in his presence.

The same emotions she experienced with Scott so many years ago.

Was she projecting the memory of how she felt about Scott onto Craig?

The question started a firestorm of doubt and confusion. Pat knew how to bring the crazy whirlwind of her thoughts under control. Inhaling long and deep, she counted her breaths in, and out, and repeated *peace be still* in her mind, until everything within her—heart, mind, and soul—calmed. Until she could think clearly.

Yes, he resembled Scott. Uncannily so. Very much aware of the power of the present moment, Pat knew, deep in her heart of hearts, she was not imposing the feelings she had for Scott so long ago onto his brother.

Mel called to fill her in on her and Garrett's latest European adventures. Before she knew it, it was time to head into Bandera. Pat ran a brush through her hair, did a quick once-over at her appearance, and left.

She arrived at the diner the same time as Craig. She stood aside and let him open the door. They sat in silence until the hostess seated them, then ordered drinks.

"So, how was your morning?"

Pat thanked the waitress when she set the drinks before them. Took a sip. "Beautiful. I've traveled to and from Mississippi several years now, and still can't get over how lovely sunrise or sunset is over these hills."

"Where in Mississippi?"

"Magnolia."

"My wife was from Greenville."

"Really? How did you meet her all the way up here?"

His wistful expression tugged at her heart. "My grandfather hired her for a summer veterinarian job."

"Interesting."

"Yeah. She passed away ten, nearly eleven years ago."

Hence, the white circle on his left hand. Had he taken his ring off since meeting her? "Sorry to hear that."

Craig acknowledged her words with a brief nod. "Thanks. How'd you know Scott?"

The waitress came over, halting the conversation. Once they placed their lunch orders, and handed her the menus, Pat answered. "I worked with him ... oh, I don't know... Thirty years ago, I guess. I'm a nurse. We were on the same mission trip in South America when his wife and parents were killed. I can't believe how much you two look alike."

Craig chuckled. "Neither could we. Rumor had it we were brothers, or at least related, but not until 2001 did we find out the truth. His mother had willed a letter for him to read upon her death, but Scott put it off for years. After 9/11, and the fact his adopted daughter and my son were expecting their first child, he decided to read it. Trina gave it to me after he died."

"What happened?"

"A strung-out drug addict in the emergency room, stabbed him. He held on for a couple of weeks but never recovered."

The hardness in his jaw and fury in his eyes convinced Pat that Craig still had a lot of raw emotions around the incident which took his brother's life. She reached across the table and put her hand over his. *To comfort, of course.* Her heart stuttered when he turned it palm up and squeezed hers before moving so the waitress could place their food on the table.

They savored their meal for a moment. "I know it's tough to lose someone you love. Melena, that's my best friend, since forever, lost her husband seven years ago. She was so broken, so vulnerable, for a long time. Even after she came to the Crossed Penn ranch—where she met Garrett—and her artistic genius flourished, it took a long while for her to really come to grips with Jon's death."

"Where's she now?"

Pat allowed the love and admiration for her friend to flow through, positive it reflected in her expression. "Honeymooning in Europe."

"Nice. So, that's what brings you here? Are you still working?"

Pat nodded. "As of now, I'm on sabbatical. Not sure if I want to continue or retire early and go in another direction. Kind of at a crossroads, I guess."

"Been there, done that. I find myself at one of those too. Ace and Lex are expecting another child soon, and the house seems to be more and more crowded."

"They live with you?"

He nodded. "Yep. Ace works part-time at the veterinarian clinic and full-time at the ranch. Lex stays busy with the two they have now. It's going to be even more hectic with a third in the mix."

"He must be the blond-haired younger version of you I saw last night."

Pat's heart did a slow swirl into her stomach at the love and pride on his face.

"Yep. My daughter is the woman..."

His words trailed off. He took a moment, it seemed, to gather his thoughts, then sighed.

"I still get choked up thinking of her as such even after three grandkids. Anyway, she's the one with long, dark hair. The others with us last night were Scott's widow Trina, their two sons and daughter, and Mike Guidry, Scott's longtime friend and colleague. They all moved here a couple years back."

Pat's lips curved. "I saw you with the smaller of the two boys a couple weeks ago on my way through."

"That's Robert, Scott's youngest. He had some after-school project, and I was already in town, so I picked him up and brought him home."

"Do they live close to you?"

"Yes. Trina and the kids live in a house I built for them between Scott's family home and my ranch. Mike lives at the B&B."

"The Hensley House B&B? I stayed there a while back. Never crossed my mind that the name had anything to do with Scott. It had been so long since I saw or even thought about him. Until I saw you two."

"Yeah. After Scott's parents and Melissa were killed, he wanted to sell the place. Tamera—that's my wife—and I convinced him to turn the home into a B&B and I bought most of the land. Left enough for trail rides and such and to host our annual charity rodeo. That way, Scott and Trina always had someplace to stay when they visited. Especially since our families grew exponentially once our two married and started having babies." He pushed his plate away and stretched back in his seat. "Enough about me. Tell me about you."

Pat shrugged. "Not much to tell. I'm a registered nurse and energy medicine practitioner. I've traveled all over the world on medical missions, seen the best and the worst of humanity. I've never married or had any children of my own but am an honorary aunt to Mel's bunch."

The conversation didn't stop. They talked through lunch and dessert. Not until he received a text message from his son, wondering where he was, did they realize the dinner crowd had started trickling in. Once again, Craig paid for her meal. They walked out together.

"This was really nice."

He stroked a hand down her arm, leaving a trail of fire lingering in its wake. "Sure was. I'd like to do it again."

Pat smiled. "Me too. I'll find my receipt."

His chuckle sent a horde of butterflies straight to her midsection. He opened her car door and waited until she'd buckled up before speaking. "You do that. Soon."

Pat backed out of the parking spot. She watched him climb into his truck, and leave, in her rearview mirror as she drove back to Garrett's cabin in Utopia.

Chapter Seven

Craig sat on the porch and sipped a glass of bourbon. He'd already hugged, kissed, and tucked his grandchildren in. He glanced down at the tablet on which he'd made notes of supplies needed to restore the cabin. The name Pat Green appeared alongside the measurements of wood to replace rotten boards. *With an e,* he thought and quickly marked through the doodling he hadn't been aware of. Just in time too. Ace walked through the door and refreshed his drink before pouring one for himself.

"How's it goin', Dad?"

"Still goin', Son." Both chortled at his dry tone.

"Not much excitement in our lives at the moment, huh?"

"Will be soon enough when that baby gets here. Lex OK?"

Ace sighed and leaned back in his chair. "Yeah. Just tired. I'll be glad when this first trimester is over. Hopefully, she'll get her second wind."

Craig refrained from commenting.

"What'cha got there?"

Craig shifted in his chair and adjusted the tablet to where his son's probing gaze couldn't read what he'd scratched out. "Some notes on what I need for the cabin."

"I rode out there today, but you were already gone. Did you order your supplies? I didn't see any in the truck."

Craig did his best to keep his expression neutral. "Went into town to do that but ran into a friend. Spent the afternoon catching up. I'll get things ordered tomorrow."

Ace nodded. Sipped. "Last night was fun. We need to do that more often."

Craig heard the unspoken question in his son's remarks. Their roles had been reversed for quite some time now. His children worried and wondered where he was, who he was with, and if he was all right. *Time for that to stop.* He decided then, and there, he'd repair or remodel the cabin and move into it as soon as humanly possible. Still, he tempered his response. "Yeah a lot of fun. Enjoyed it more than I thought, considering how tired I was."

"That's good. Once you get what all you need to fix the cabin, we can rally the troops and get it done in a jiffy."

Craig hadn't been this excited over a project since he built Trina's home. But, in all honesty, he wanted to do this alone. "We'll see. Lots of cleaning and prep work before then."

Before Ace could respond, Craig's cellphone signaled an incoming text message. He glanced at the screen, slipped the device back into his shirt pocket, and rose.

"Something important?"

No way in hell would he discuss this with his son. Not yet anyway. *Can't lie to him either.* He tucked the tablet beneath his arm and searched his mind for the right words and tone of voice. "Just my friend thanking me for lunch. Gonna call it a night. I'm about done in."

"I'm not far behind you. 'Night, Daddy."

Craig squeezed his son's shoulder on his way into the house.

* * *

Ace sat alone for long moments after his father went inside. Hope curled in his heart that Craig might actually begin to find his way back to truly living again. He took a deep breath, fought back a surge of tears, and swallowed the lump in his throat. *Oh, Mama. If you have any pull up there, send someone to fill his life with joy. We've missed our* real *daddy for so long.*

Her presence surrounded him. Ace smelled the earthy perfume she always wore. Felt her arms around him as though she were physically there. He heard her voice reassure him his father is, and would continue to be, fine.

When the essence of her visit faded, he followed in his father's footsteps and went to bed. He held his wife as close as was comfortable for her in her present condition and loved her deep into the night.

* * *

Craig got ready for bed before opening his phone to read Pat's message.

Hey Cowboy. Found my receipt. Smiley-faced emoji. *Thank you for a lovely afternoon. Here's my number. Now you can continue the pursuit. If you've a mind to. Good night.* Sleepy emoji.

Oh, I've a mind to.

A happy-faced emoji was her answer to his response. Grabbing the tablet off his bedside table, he turned to a fresh page, and sketched the additions he planned for the cabin.

The one-room efficiency would soon become a two-bedroom, two-bath, bungalow. He'd convert the current sleeping area into an open living/dining room and add a utility closet. Ideas for a front porch and back deck flowed onto the subsequent pages. He worked late into the night until the plans were planted firmly in his mind.

The following morning, he woke with fire in his soul and purpose in his heart. He glanced through the tablet and added a few more notes to what he'd already done. He knew the original structure's square footage and figured he'd simply double its size. He calculated the amount of lumber, along with other items, he'd need for the addition. Dressing, he tugged on boots, grabbed his hat, and made his way downstairs, where daily chaos ensued.

Ace urged Tamera to hurry and finish breakfast so they could head out to school and the vet clinic. "'Morning, Dad. Trina will be here afterwhile to watch the baby. Would you mind hanging around until she gets here?"

"Not at all." The relief on his son's face won out against the quick surge of irritation at having his plans for the morning thwarted. *This too shall pass,* Craig repeated over and over in his mind, reminding himself that Lexie was only a couple of weeks away from reaching the second trimester of this pregnancy.

Less than an hour later, Trina knocked on the kitchen door and entered, bringing a blast of icy air in with her. "Whew, looks like winter might make an early appearance. Turned colder overnight."

Craig glanced at the temperature gauge on the wall.

The reading showed a drop of several degrees from the day before. He kissed Trina's cheek. "Guess I'll run upstairs and grab another layer of clothing in case I need them."

Trina acknowledged his comment with a smile and nod and moved to tend to their grandson.

Craig went to his room, tossed a long-sleeved T-shirt and sweater into a backpack, and threw in an extra pair of socks. He exited in time to meet Trina backing out of Ace and Lexie's door, her expression frozen with worry. "How is she?"

Trina swallowed hard and shook her head. "I'm concerned. She doesn't seem to be pulling out of this morning sickness as well as she did with the other two. I'm going to ask Mike to come over and check on her later."

"Good. I'll be out at the old hunting cabin. Doing some repairs and remodeling. Should have cell service, so call if you need anything. Everyone knows how to find me if you can't reach me."

"No problem. Be careful out there all alone."

"Will do. See you later." Craig called the friend who'd helped him finalize plans, draw blueprints, and get permits, when he'd built Trina's home, and asked to meet him at the cabin, then gave instructions on how to get there. Loading the tractor onto a trailer, he headed there himself. Chip arrived within the hour as agreed. The two walked around the structure while Craig explained his plans.

"Shouldn't be a problem to do this, Craig. But..." He climbed the ladder Craig had brought out the day before. "You're going to need a whole new roof soon. Might want to consider adding a loft while you're at it."

"Why would I need a loft?"

He grinned. "Because as soon as you move out here, those grandkids are going to want to come stay with you and bring friends."

Craig considered the suggestion, adjusted his hat, and heaved a breath. "You're probably right. Add that in."

They continued to talk, take measurements, and share ideas, while Chip sketched more professional versions of Craig's initial drawings. "I'll finish the material list, and blueprints, for you by Monday."

"Thanks. What time should I come by and get them?"

Chip looked at the calendar on his phone and offered a couple of options. Before Craig could answer, his cell rang. Katrina's face flashed on the screen. Craig accepted the call. "Hey, Trina. What's up?"

He nodded and waved at Chip when the man said, "see ya later," and walked toward his vehicle.

"Mike can't come out, so I'm taking Lexie to the clinic. I'll drop Little Ace off with Amber, but can you get the kids from school? Stanley is waiting on a client to come get a horse."

"Sure."

"Thanks."

"No worries." Craig ended the conversation, looked at his watch, and determined he only had a couple of hours to get some work done. He climbed up on the tractor and commenced clearing the brush around the cabin and making room for the additions.

At two o'clock, he shut things down, went back to the

house to shower and change, and left to pick up the kids.

Later that evening, after everyone else was in bed, he reread Pat's message from the previous night and texted her.

Hope you had a great day and evening. Sweet dreams.

When a reply didn't come right away, he put the phone aside, and fell into one of the most restful slumbers he'd experienced in a long time.

The first thing he did upon waking was check his phone. She'd answered and his heart thrilled at her response.

Chapter Eight

Pat heard her phone jingle indicating a message had come through. *Wonder if that's him?* She pulled her mind back and focused on her breath and movements. *He can wait. Don't want to appear too anxious.*

Although she was. Uncharacteristically so.

Losing her balance, Pat hissed in a gulp of air, and reeled in her thoughts once more. No way was she going to let this, *or any,* man interrupt her daily routine. Specifically, one who couldn't seem to dial her number.

Text messaging was all fine and well, but she preferred to have a conversation... audibly... face to face. And after the one they shared two days ago, followed by a whole day without contact, she had no idea how to act. Or what to think. She had no clue how dating worked in this day and age. *So out of practice.*

Yoga complete, she sat down to meditate but couldn't stop the whirlwind of thoughts in her head. She retrieved her phone and read what appeared to be a message from last night. Closing her eyes, she listened to her heart, and answered...

Morning, Cowboy. Just received your message. Had a wonderful day and evening and sweet dreams indeed. WYD today?

Excitement raced through her when he answered that he had a full day of work but was free for dinner.

Before she could respond, Melena called. "Hey, Mel."

"So, how's it going? Have you seen him again?"

Pat told her of their dancing on Wednesday night

and four-hour lunch on Thursday. "He mentioned being free for dinner tonight, but I'm not sure if that's an invitation or a hint."

Melena squealed. "Invite him over!"

"You don't think that's too forward? Too much, too soon?"

"Girl, these days, women sometimes have to take the initiative."

"Yeah. Maybe. When will y'all be home?"

"I talked to my kids, and we'll have a late Thanksgiving celebration, so Garrett and I can stay another week. Hope you're there too."

"That's great, Mel. I'm not sure yet what I'm doing. Might see if Anne needs help. But I'll definitely be home when y'all get there."

"She probably wouldn't turn you down. Garrett says 'hi' and feel free to continue staying in the cabin. We won't be heading back there until after Christmas."

"Tell him 'thanks.' I appreciate that. Y'all have fun."

"We will," Mel replied and rang off.

Taking her friend's advice, Pat opened Craig's message again and typed... *Since you've bought me dinner* and *lunch, how about I treat you this time?*

A shy-faced emoji came before... *A treat I'm sure it would be. But I'm not used to letting a lady pay for my meal.*

Pat shoved aside her egoic response to that and answered. *OK then, how about I cook you dinner?*

Her heart pounded.

Now that sounds like a plan. Where? What time? What can I bring?"

She texted back the address, time, and *just your*

appetite, then did a little dance around the cabin. Digging through the freezer, panic set in. What in the hell am I thinking? I have no idea what the man likes or doesn't like!

Calm down, Pat. She chided herself mentally. The man's a rancher, for goodness sakes. He'll probably eat pretty much anything.

Pat decided she'd sauté chicken breasts surrounded by new potatoes and green beans and serve that along with a green salad, crescent rolls, and a pumpkin pie. Satisfied with her menu, she headed to the grocery store to get the ingredients she couldn't find stocked in Garrett's kitchen.

She put the breasts in a marinating sauce then spent the afternoon reading. At five o'clock, she put the meal on to cook, prepared the salad, and then changed from sweats, into jeans and a sweater. The rolls were ready to go into the oven after Craig arrived–which he did at precisely 5:45–carrying a bottle of red wine.

He stepped through the door and looked around. "Nice cabin."

Pat opened the wine to let it breathe a moment or two. "Thanks. This belongs to Melena's husband. They're not coming back for a few months, so I'm free to stay until then."

He took her hand and raised it to his lips. "I hope you stay longer than that."

Heat suffused her face. Pat disengaged her hand from his with a tiny laugh. "We'll see."

"Shall I pour?"

Pat nodded. "Glasses are in that little cabinet over there." She pointed. "Corkscrew in the drawer beneath.

I'll put the rolls in to bake. Make yourself comfortable."

Craig found the items he needed, opened the wine, and poured two glasses. "This place reminds me of the hunting cabin on my ranch. Except it'll be much larger before long."

Pat raised a brow at him. "Oh?"

Craig nodded. Sipped. "Yeah, doing a bit of remodeling."

"That's good. I guess."

He sat on the couch, stretched those incredibly long legs, and took another taste of his wine. "Going to turn it into a home for myself. Time for me to have some space of my own."

The look he sent her had shimmers racing up and down her spine. Pat eased her suddenly dry throat with a gulp of wine. "How do your children feel about that?"

"Haven't told them yet. They know I'm working out there but have no idea as to the extent of what I plan to do."

"I'm sure they'll be surprised."

He agreed. "Probably a bit relieved, too."

Pat set the table and asked his preference of drink for dinner. He raised his glass in salute. "This'll be fine."

Pat removed the rolls, placed them in a basket and set it beside the other cookware piled with food. "Great. We'll have coffee with dessert later."

She waited until he pulled a chair out for her before sitting, and until he was seated with his napkin in his lap, before serving. As it had two days ago, conversation flowed between them. He talked about his ranch and his family.

She told stories of the many medical missions she'd

been on, how much she adored Melena and her family, and showed him pictures of some of their artwork.

After dinner, they moved into the living room and talked more. When she got up to serve the pie and coffee, he rinsed and stacked the plates and silverware into the dishwasher. They returned to their seats, and enjoyed the dessert, while continuing to chat. The clock struck ten. They looked at each other in astonishment at how quickly the evening passed and the total ease they felt together.

Craig rose from the couch with obvious hesitancy. "Guess I'd better head on out of here."

Her own reluctance at his leaving filled her with even more surprise, but she waited while he carried their saucers and cups to the kitchen sink. "Leave them. I'll finish loading the dishwasher, and turn it on, before I go to bed."

The longing in his eyes when he turned to face her once more, stole the air right out of her lungs. Pat hesitated a moment, then walked to where he stood and put her arms around his waist. She rested her head against his heart, glad when he completed the embrace with a brush of his lips across her head.

"Thank you for coming. I had a lovely evening."

"Me too. We're having our usual family gathering tomorrow at the ranch. Would you like to join us?"

Pat gazed at him and saw the hint of uncertainty shining alongside the hope in his eyes. She moved out of his arms, stepped back, and smiled to hide her mixed emotions. "I'd love to, but I've got other plans tomorrow. Perhaps another time."

Craig acknowledged her answer with an incline of

his head. They walked toward the door. He turned and cupped her face in his hands. She saw the question in his eyes this time, and raised up on her tiptoes, to touch her lips to his cheek. "Next time."

Before she could pull away, he gathered her close, clung, pressed a brief kiss to her lips, and then walked down the steps. Pat waited until he'd opened his truck door and hollered for him to let her know he made it home safely. "I might not get the message until tomorrow. Service is sometimes delayed out here. But please let me know anyway."

His grin did that funny thing with her insides. "Will do. 'Night."

Pat bid him goodnight, closed the door, finished loading the dishwasher, and then got ready for bed. His text came as she crawled beneath the covers...

Home safe. Thanks again for the wonderful meal and great company. Let's do it again.

Soon.

We will, she replied.

The next day, she rode out to the Crossed Penn to volunteer her services for the following week.

Chapter Nine

Craig rolled out of bed with a groan. Fall had flown in with a vengeance, and the weather turned frigid overnight. These old bones like the cold less and less, he thought, standing a long time under a warm shower. His plans for the week had already gone awry. *And it's only Monday.*

The kids were out of school. Lexie still hadn't jumped the hurdle of her first trimester. And he'd be busy helping out as much as possible. Meaning he wouldn't get every bit of the work he'd wanted to do, on the cabin, done.

There's always a way.

The words whispered through his mind. Ideas began to flow. His teenaged twin granddaughters were old enough to entertain the younger girls. Amber and her son would be delighted to help with Little Ace, and Scott's two boys, could lend him a hand. It'll cost a pretty penny to hire out their services, he thought with a grimace. But worth every cent.

He finished his shower, and lined things up for the next couple of days. Satisfied, he headed into Bandera to pick up the material list and blueprints. Permits were forthcoming. *If* not delayed by the Thanksgiving holiday. Craig made a mental note to stop by the courthouse.

Now, where to fit Pat in? Memories of Saturday night warmed his soul the same way the hot water had eased the chill out of his body. He'd agreed to give the kids this day off since their school holiday break had just begun. So... Breakfast? Maybe lunch.

He dialed her number, disappointed when her

phone went to voicemail. *Damn.* He *hated* leaving messages. When the beep sounded, he cleared his throat and said, "Good Morning. It's Craig. Hope I don't wake you or anything. I'm going to be in Bandera most of the day. Hope we can meet up at some point. Give me a call. OK. Bye for now."

Oh well, since he'd left the ranch before eating–because he'd wanted his call to be private–he'd grab something at some point. A half-hour later, her call came in. "Hello."

"Morning, Cowboy. Lunch sounds lovely. Same time, same place?"

"No. Let's go somewhere different. Meet me at the café behind the motel on 16. We can sit out by the river. You know which one I'm talking about?"

"Sure do. One o'clock?"

"Yep. Dress warm."

"Will do. See you in a while."

"Looking forward to it." Oh, how he hoped he didn't sound like an over-anxious teenager. Which is exactly how he felt.

He stopped at the highway intersection, closed his eyes, and listened for Tamera's voice telling him, once again, that it was OK for him to have another woman in his life. The depth of her love flowed through him–mind, body, and soul–leaving no doubt she wanted this for him. He fingered the cross and ring on the chain around his neck and continued the drive into town.

At 12:50, he parked his truck, entered the restaurant, and searched the crowd for her face. When he turned to go back outside to wait, she drove up. Joy flooded his entire being followed by the swift kick of desire. He opened the door with a flourish. "Hey."

The light in her eyes curled through him like a caress. "Hi."

Heat zinged through his fingertips when he placed a hand on her back and escorted her to a table. Once seated and their orders in, he leaned forward and took her hand. "How was your day, yesterday?"

"Nice. Quiet. I drove out to the Crossed Penn and visited with the folks there. I'll be working Wednesday through Sunday."

"Doing what?"

Pat shrugged. "Cooking. Cleaning. Serving. Riding. Whatever needs to be done. They're always packed this time of year. With Garrett, and Melena, out of the country, and Missy pregnant, I thought I'd help out."

"Sounds exhausting."

She laughed. "Yeah. But in a good way. I enjoy physical labor. Occasionally."

He chuckled. "Physical labor is par for the course in my line of work. Although, I haven't been as actively involved in the day-to-day for a while."

"How's the family?"

Craig sat back and waited until the waitress put their meals on the table to answer. "Good. Boisterous. Lexie is still battling morning sickness. We're all a bit worried about that. But her doctor reports are all fine."

"Lexie... that's your daughter-in-law. Right?"

He nodded.

"And Scott's...?"

"Adopted daughter. She came into their lives as a foster child when she was... I don't know, twelve or thirteen. Her father died a few years afterward. Scott and

Trina adopted her. I'll never forget the first time she and Ace met. Like a match to a fuse," he said with a laugh. "Much like my first encounter with Tamera."

Pat grinned. "I'd love to hear all about that."

Craig cocked his head. "Really? I thought women didn't want to know about the previous relationships in their man's life."

He'd have given all of his wealth to capture her expression on film… The way her eyes lit up and cheeks flushed. The kaleidoscope of emotions, that flitted across her face. Awe. Wonder. Hope.

"Are you my man?"

"I'd like to be. But perhaps we're getting too far ahead of ourselves."

She fidgeted charmingly. Sipped her water. "Perhaps. So, tell me about Tamera."

Over lunch, he told her how he'd met the one woman who'd stolen his heart by having no problem putting him in his place. Her fiery personality, gentle spirit, and extraordinary gift with horses. Everything. Including how her death tore his world apart. A world he was just now feeling the urge to rebuild.

Pat wiped tears off her cheeks and reached over to take his hand. "What a beautiful testament. Any man who loves, honors, and cherishes his wife so completely more than a decade after her death, deserves a second chance to live with that kind of love again."

Craig knuckled the moisture from his eyes. "I never thought I'd want to. My kids have nagged me for years to move on, but I don't know how. Or thought I didn't. These last few days with you have shown me differently. And no matter where our friendship goes from here, I will be forever grateful to you for that."

He watched her throat convulse. She swallowed hard and took another drink. "I never thought I'd want to fall in love or settle down. Traveling and nursing are in my blood. But lately, I'd been feeling... Lost, I guess. And envious of my best friend. Melena had a beautiful marriage and has found that depth of love a second time. Made me wonder if I'd missed out on something. When I saw you with the boy... Robert, right?"

Craig nodded.

"And thought you were Scott. I realized why that was. In all the years and the few, very few, exclusive relationships I'd been in, I hadn't met a man with the intensity of character Scott exhibited in the short time we'd worked together. Oh, they were some great guys, but we always seemed to outgrow one another. Mentally, emotionally, or spiritually."

She shrugged. "Might sound crazy, but I just knew, somewhere deep in my soul, that I hadn't found the right person yet. That I might never. That he was one of a kind."

"And now?"

A pulsating pause stretched between them. "Now, I have hope."

Craig signaled the waitress for the check. "Hope's always a good thing. What are you doing the rest of the day?"

Pat lifted her shoulders and eyebrows at the same time.

"Wanna take a drive?"

"Sure."

He paid the tab, and they took off in his truck. Thirty

minutes down the road, Craig pulled into one of the many entrances onto his ranch and stopped. "If you'll drive on through, it'll save us a few minutes."

Pat slid over into the seat he vacated and did as he asked. She crossed back to the passenger side once he'd closed the gate behind them. Craig glanced at her. "No need to buckle up, now. We're on private property."

"Where are we going?"

"I want to show you what I'm working on."

"Your cabin? This is your ranch?"

"Yeah. The Rockin' H. Been in my family for generations."

"Oh, wow. I've heard so much about it. And you."

He grimaced. "Not all positive, I'm sure."

She giggled. "I don't listen to idle gossip. But one thing's for certain, people respect you and what you've done out here. With this place."

"That's good to know."

Another thirty minutes or so, he stopped the truck, disembarked, and hurried around to open her door. A sigh of pure appreciation escaped her lips as Pat climbed down and surveyed the cabin surrounded by woods. "Oh, man, this is..."

"A mess. I know."

She grinned in response to his teasing.

"But it won't be for long."

He removed the blueprints from the truck's back seat and walked with her into the dimly lit building, cautioning her to be careful. Unrolling the plans, he pointed out changes and improvements as they moved throughout and around the perimeters. They exited as a truck rolled into view.

A surge of fear, followed by panic, filled his entire being, obliterating any thoughts he'd had of being 'her man.' He frowned. "Wonder what he's doing here?"

Thank God he's alone.

Chapter Ten

Tension filled the air. Crawled up her spine. Pat edged away from Craig as the driver, whom she recognized as one of his family members, got out of the vehicle.

"Stanley?" Craig's tone had a ring to it that grated on her suddenly taut nerves.

"We've been trying to reach you. Amber got worried. So, here I am." Stanley's voice reeked with surprise and contrition.

Craig cleared his throat and turned to face her, his expression alive with mixed feelings. Fear. Panic. Resignation. He tried to smile. Failed.

Miserably.

"This is Pat Greene." He glanced from her to the younger man. "My son-in-law, Stanley Morrison."

The young man tipped his hat and held a hand out to her. Pat shook it. "Nice to meet you."

The excitement and admiration in his eyes could have melted ice off a glacier. "Likewise. Well, guess I'll let Amber know everything is OK out here."

He pivoted on his heel and climbed back into his SUV.

Craig followed. "Stan... Uh..." He looked her way. Lowered his voice. Still, she heard... "I just met her so..."

Pat whirled away, stormed into Craig's truck, slammed the door, and wished to hell she'd followed instead of riding with him. She watched their animated discussion for a moment, then turned away. Blinked back fury.

Stanley's truck roared off. The cabin door shut with

a bang. Craig flung the blueprints onto his back seat, yanked the driver's door open, lunged behind the wheel, and started the vehicle.

A noxious cloud accompanied them to the edge of the drive. He didn't ask her to slide over and pull the truck through the gate this time. Which was a good thing since she'd probably leave him standing in the dust of his own property. His entrance into the truck was a lot more restrained than before. He heaved in a breath, two, and dry-washed his face with his hands.

"Look. I'm sorry. I know I didn't handle that very well."

No shit, Sherlock. Pat ground her teeth to keep from lashing out. They drove back to where she'd left her car in strained silence. She didn't wait for him to be the gentleman this time, but wrenched the door ajar, and barreled out, the minute he rolled to a stop. "Thank you for the apology, but know this, I will not be your dirty little secret."

In one fluid movement, she closed his door with a thump and tugged her's open. Before she could escape, he grabbed her arm. Pat stiffened and refrained from jerking away. "Don't you dare manhandle me," she spit out between clenched teeth.

Craig removed his hand and backed away, both palms held up in a gesture of peace. "Never. I'm really sorry. Please... Don't..."

His inability to articulate a complete sentence did absolutely nothing to endear him to her at the moment. "You said that already. For someone who has talked with me for *hours* every time we're together, you seem to be at a loss for words."

Temper sparked in his steely gaze. Every feeling she'd seen on his face throughout the whole crazy incident, exploded in an instant. "I don't know what the fff..." He bit off the word with a hiss. "Hell, to say! Go ahead. Drive off in a snit. I thought we were adults here. Guess not."

Years of being a healer, and living life from a heart filled with compassion, didn't stop the surge of anger and insult spewing through her veins. *"You're* the one acting like a kid caught with his hand stuck in the cookie jar!"

The conviction in her tone, mixed with the humor in her choice of words, hit them simultaneously.

He grinned.

She giggled.

Craig stepped in and swept her against his chest. His hands journeyed over her back in a restless motion. "It's just... I'm... This is all so new to me. So, unexpected. I'd appreciate it if you give me a chance, some time, to figure it out."

Her pent-up emotions escaped in a woosh of breath. Pat wrapped her arms around his waist and lifted her chin. Her quip halted at the intensity of his gaze. Lips curved at the array of sentiments glinting in those gray gems. "You're a strong, enigmatic man, Craig. I can't believe you're afraid of the children you brought into this world."

He smiled as she hoped he would.

"You don't know my kids."

"I'd like to."

"You will. Soon."

Pat pressed her lips to his cheek. "I'll hold you to that, Cowboy."

Craig moved his hand from the middle of her back to cradle her skull. He cuddled her a moment, then shifted and covered her lips in a kiss so... Tender. Devastating. *Those strong arms...Hard body.* Her head began to spin. Heart pounded. Blood sang in her ears. Muscles quivered. Bones liquified. Her knees threatened to buckle, so she tightened her grip on him. *It's a good thing he's holding me. Otherwise, he'd have to scrape me off the concrete with his pocketknife.*

When she could hardly breathe, much less think, he ended the embrace in slow degrees.

"How about Wednesday night?"

"What about it?"

He laughed. "Meet my kids. Wednesday night."

"I already told you I'm working at the Crossed Penn this week. I doubt I'll be able to get away until after the weekend."

"Shoot. OK. Next week, then. I'll call."

"You do that. But make it quick, Cowboy. I'm leaving next Wednesday to head back to Mississippi. Melena and Garrett will be home the following weekend, and the family is having a late Thanksgiving celebration with them."

"Monday or Tuesday it is. I'll let you know as soon as I know."

"Ok."

One more kiss, and they went their separate ways.

* * *

Stanley took the long way home. Drove as slowly as

possible. Argued with himself the entire way. He couldn't–wouldn't–lie to his wife. But he knew her all too well and understood his father-in-law's desire for discretion. The fact Craig had even ventured into a tentative friendship with another woman would be fodder for Amber's imagination. She and Ace would be all over that like the proverbial flies on manure. No one would get a moment's peace until Craig was safely settled into another relationship. Or whatever his well-meaning but over protective, and sometimes overbearing, children wanted.

"God...Tam...help me here..."

As usual, when he sought guidance, direction or reassurance, his mother-in-law's presence surrounded him with love, and peace, so tangible, he'd swear she sat beside him.

"Don't tell her, Stanley. Not yet."

He heard the words as clearly as he would have, had she actually occupied the adjacent seat. "Then help me answer her questions without having to out-and-out lie."

"Just reassure her he's fine. No more. No less."

He stopped in his driveway. Adjusted his hat. Checked the mirror to be sure his expression was as neutral as possible. Putting a smile on his face, and a whistle on his lips, he exited the truck. He walked onto the porch, through the house, and into the kitchen, where his wife stared forlornly out the window.

She turned to him. "Well?"

"He's fine, Amber. Out at the cabin. You know how spotty the signal can be out there."

Her shoulders sagged with relief. "I'm so worried about him. The other night, when that lady kept looking at him, I'd hoped he'd at least ask her to dance."

"Who knows, maybe he did. Ace said he got home late. Either way, it's none of our business. Unless *he* makes it so."

Irritation flashed in the sapphire eyes he loved so much. "He *is* my business."

Stanley gathered her into his arms. "No, My Sweet. He's your father. Remember the talk we had right after William was born? About letting him get through this in his own way, own time?"

She nodded.

"He's working on the cabin, Amber. That's something in and of itself. Whether he decides to live there, or simply creates a place he can escape to, he's making an effort to move forward. Let him do that. At...His...Own...Pace," he muttered, nibbling on the corners of her mouth to distract her.

Didn't work.

"It's just... We've lost so much. I'm afraid we'll lose him, too, if he doesn't pull out of this. Long before it's time. Long before I'm ready."

Stanley captured her tears with his lips. "We won't lose him, My Sweet." He eyed her with a stern look. Well, as stern as he could ever be with her.

"Unless we push him away." He caressed her back and shoulders and whispered his love, then grinned when one of his daughters walked into the room and rolled her eyes at them.

"Ugh. You two need to get a room."

Stan laughed. "We've got one. Gonna close your eyes and cover your ears?"

Kaitlyn turned several shades of red and pretended

to gag.

Stanley reached out and dragged her into their embrace. Within minutes, his other daughter, and son, ambled into the room, and a wrestling match ensued. Until Amber shoved the lot of them out the back door while she finished preparing dinner.

Chapter Eleven

Craig followed Pat out of the parking lot, turning right when she turned left. *Almost screwed that up.* Fear spiraled through him at the thought. What if she got home and reconsidered? What if she never spoke to him again? Even after that kiss.

He couldn't make himself believe what they shared in their first, full meeting of mouths, was one-sided. Still, she'd been furious.

And hurt.

And *that* was unacceptable.

He spotted a place off the shoulder, where he could stop his truck, and dig his cellphone out of his pocket. Before he could dial Pat's number, it rang. Amber's face flashed on the screen. *Dear God, please don't let Stanley have told her anything.*

"Hello?"

"Hey, Daddy. You OK?"

Craig swallowed the growl rising in his throat. He was so tired of that question—Every. Single. Time. One of his children called. "I'm fine. What'cha need?"

"William wants to help you, and the boys, instead of playing with the *b-a-by,* as he so eloquently sneered a moment ago."

Craig chuckled at the amusement in her voice. "I'm sure I can find something for him to do. Either let him spend the night at Trina's, or have her boys stay with you. That way, I can pick them all up at one place. We'll start around eight-thirty in the morning."

"Trina's already on her way to get him and bringing Little Ace to me. Rikki is staying with Tamera Joy tonight."

"Good deal."

"Have you had supper yet?"

"No."

"Stop by. We're about to sit down, but we'll wait, if you'd like to eat with us."

Craig hesitated. The last thing he wanted to do was face Stanley after their tense conversation earlier. *Coward.* Maybe so, but he needed some time, and space, to unwind, and think, before facing his brood. "No thanks, sweetheart. Pack William enough clothes for a couple of days, and I'll see y'all tomorrow or Wednesday. The boys and I'll take Thursday and the weekend off so I want to get as much work out of them as I can. While I can."

"Slave driver."

Craig laughed at the teasing in her tone. "They gotta learn some time."

They ended the conversation, and he turned his truck back toward the cabin. He'd have to use a spotlight to see anything out there this late, but he wanted to bask in thoughts of the better parts of his day. He grabbed the battery-operated device out of his tool box, checked the charge, turned it on, and waved it over the ground as he walked toward the cabin.

Memories crowded his mind as he picked his way through the deteriorating structure. Some good. Others, not. He remembered when his grandfather found his parents here. Dead. His and Tamera's honeymoon. The time he discovered Amber, and Stanley, holed up after they'd been caught in a summer storm while out riding.

The more he walked around, the more he realized

what terrible shape the entire thing was in. The refrigerator and dishes had long since been removed, and electricity cut off. Cabinet doors hung on rusty hinges. Floors creaked. Windows rattled. Something fell. Craig ran the ray of light along a beam from the ceiling and escaped before it completely collapsed. To hell with repairing and remodeling. Tomorrow, he, and the boys, would begin tearing this thing down, and he'd start over. Build anew.

New cabin.

New life.

He returned to his truck, opened the door to climb in, and hesitated. A flash of movement caught the corner of his eye. A coyote yipped in the distance. Owl hooted. A breeze rustled the trees. Leaves showered down around him. Slowly, quietly and with as little noise as possible, he flickered the light toward the sounds. A huge, white-tailed buck stood not fifteen feet from the hood of his truck. Frozen like a statue from the bright beam aimed in his eyes.

The sight of the majestic animal filled his soul with awe and wonder. Craig turned off the light, waited until he heard the stag bound into the woods, and then clambered into the cab. He drove away, carefully watching in case another deer jumped out of the brush. As soon as he got a good cell signal, he called Chip. "Hey, buddy. I know it's late, and I'm sorry to bother you, but about those plans you drew for me?"

He paused when Chip responded, then continued. "Trash'em. I'm starting over from scratch. Same design we discussed. All new construction."

They talked for a few minutes, then Craig meandered

on home. He arrived in time to catch two little girls racing down the stairs. Screeching laughter rang out when they noticed him.

"PaPaw!"

"Uncle Craig!"

He squatted as they flew into his embrace and scooped each one up in an arm. "How're my girls tonight?"

"We're playing hide and seek with Daddy," Tamera Joy squealed.

Rikki rubbed the stubble on his cheek and sniffed. "Ugh, you smell and need a shave."

Tamera did the same on the other side of his face. "Yeah. Scruffy."

"Scruffy, huh? I'll show you scruffy." He growled and nibbled on both tender necks until shrieks and giggles filled the air.

Ace jogged down the stairs, tagged each girl, and then told them to get ready for bed.

"How's Lexie tonight?"

"She's actually really good. Had a great day. Not much nausea at all. Hopefully, she'll be able to enjoy Thanksgiving dinner, and get on with the rest of this pregnancy much easier."

"Hope so."

"You going to join me outside? I'll grab a glass and bottle of... What do you want to drink tonight?"

Craig shook his head. "Think I'll head on to bed. I've been informed I'm smelly, scruffy, and need a shave."

Ace's laughter followed him into his room.

Once settled into his bed, Craig opened his phone, hoping to have a message from Pat. Disappointed that he didn't, and unsure if he should contact her or give her some space after today, he decided on the latter and turned off the lamp. Sleep, when it came wasn't restful.

The following morning, he drove to Trina's house and picked up his helpers. The four headed to the cabin, where he provided gloves, goggles, and hardhats for each of them.

"Man, this place is a dump."

Craig handed Richard a sledge hammer. "Yep. Which is why we're going to tear it down. I'll knock it over with the tractor, then we'll start cutting it up."

"What are we going to do?" Robert wanted to know.

"You two are going to wait here, by the truck, until we get it down. Then you'll haul wood out of the way." He hesitated, looked around, and pointed to an area, bare of grass from the clearing he'd done last week. "Over there. We'll pile it up and, when we're done, have a big bonfire."

"All right!" They chimed in unison.

The difference in age and size doesn't hinder the excitement of wrecking something, Craig thought with a grin and vaulted onto the tractor. "Put on your goggles and stand back. This'll bust the glass out of those windows. It's liable to fly everywhere."

Richard stood back with Robert, and William, and watched him bulldoze the house off its blocks, to the ground. He parked the tractor, jumped off it, and asked Richard to bring him the chainsaw. "Bust up what you can. I'll cut. We'll call you two over when we're ready for you to start hauling."

By the time they broke for lunch, then worked late into the afternoon, William had given up and sat on the truck's tailgate, nursing his blistered hands. Robert grunted and heaved as he dragged a log to the ever-growing pile. Young and robust, Richard could have gone on for hours. But Craig found himself about as worn out as the two youngsters.

They'd barely finished loading the tools when Amber, and Stanley, arrived carrying a platter of fried chicken, french fries, rolls, and jugs of tea. The boys jumped on the food like ravenous wolves on a fresh kill.

"I thought you were going to clean it up and repair or remodel."

Craig bit into a piece of breast, reminisced a minute over his dinner with Pat three days ago, then addressed his daughter. "Realized that was out of the question when a ceiling beam nearly hit me on the head."

"Which is *why* you don't need to be here alone," his daughter interjected.

"Not a problem now." He nodded toward the east. "Going to clear a few acres. Maybe dig a pond. Not sure yet, what all I'm going to do. But it's time for a change. And time for me to get out from under Ace, and Lexie's, feet."

"Does Ace know that?"

"No, but he will. Soon enough."

Chapter Twelve

Thanksgiving dawned bright and clear. And colder than he remembered it ever being. He, and the boys, didn't get as much work done yesterday as he'd wanted, or as much as they'd accomplished Tuesday. A winter storm had rolled in bringing with it an icy chill and the possibility of sleet. Potentially snow. Which he seriously doubted. It hadn't snowed in November as far back as he could remember.

Still, the mere chance thrilled the kids, but had the opposite effect on the adults who prayed they wouldn't face schools closing for more than this scheduled week. Other than a couple of texts, he hadn't heard from Pat. She'd reiterated how busy they were. And how tired she was as a result.

He smiled to himself at her latest message.

Even *occasionally* enjoying physical labor has its limits.

I hear ya, he replied.

He stayed in his room as long as feasible without being sought out, hoping she'd be able to respond. With the weather, locations, and distance between the two ranches, the chance of her having a decent signal was slim to none. Resigned that he'd hear from her when he heard from her, he dressed and went downstairs.

The family started trickling in around mid-morning bringing side dishes, desserts, and drinks to go with the ham Lexie baked, and the turkey Ace fried. Grownups filled the large dining table chairs. Kids occupied the smaller ones in the kitchen.

Conversation ebbed and flowed as dishes were

passed around, plates filled, and meals savored. *Bustin' at the seams.* Even with his heart exploding with gratitude, the ache in Craig's chest, over those missing, throbbed like a sore tooth. His cellphone chimed, signaling an incoming text. Before he could excuse himself, Amber gave him a questioning gaze and looked at her brother.

"Wonder what happened to no cellphones at the table?"

Ace winked at her and turned an inquisitive eye to him. "My sentiments, exactly."

Craig grunted. "What happened to 'do as I say, not as I do'?" He pushed his chair back. "Besides, I'm the oldest at this table *and* the patriarch of this family. That allows me the privilege to bend, break, or rewrite, whichever rules I please."

"A text message on Thanksgiving Day. You can bet that's not business," Amber remarked, as he strode from the room.

* * *

Stanley suppressed a groan. *Here we go…*

"You think he's met someone and is keeping it a secret?" Trina asked.

Mike's voice joined in the fray. "You think that's why he's working on the cabin all of a sudden?"

Stanley scooted his chair away from the table and stood. "Maybe he doesn't want everybody in his business just yet."

"That's ridiculous," his wife retorted, then narrowed her eyes. "Wait. What do you mean by that? You know something we don't?"

Stan picked his plate up and turned on his heel so she wouldn't see the guilt swarming through him, reflected on his face. "I know the man has a right to his privacy. Especially from those who love and worry about him the most."

He left their animated discussion behind and escaped through the kitchen.

* * *

Craig ignored the voices coming from the dining room, as they volleyed, back, and forth, over what his message meant. He accessed the phone with his thumbprint. A huge turkey sporting a "Happy Thanksgiving" banner pranced across the screen followed by...

Hey Cowboy. Hope you're having a lovely day. Some of the guests are leaving early so I'll be free sooner than I thought. I have a hot date with a whirlpool and sauna on Saturday. But I'm available for dinner if you are.

Whirlpool? Sauna? He'd love to see her lounging in a bathing suit or... Heat balled in his gut like a tight fist and spread from there. Scorching his veins. Searing his cheeks. He bolted out to the porch, hoping the cold would ease the sting of needs he'd denied for so long.

Stanley walked around from the back. "Speculations are flyin' now."

"I'll take care of that."

"Make it soon. I won't lie to my wife if she asks another direct question."

Craig hesitated in responding to Pat and laid a hand on his son-in-law's shoulder. "Wouldn't ask you to. I'm sorry if it seemed like I did. Thank you for your discretion so far."

"This woman... You think she's someone special? Or can be?"

Hope and fear collided in Stanley's gaze. Craig hesitated a moment, closed his eyes, and answered from his heart. "I've known her the whole of two weeks, but, yeah, I think she might. I know this much. She is the first spark of interest I've felt since Tamera died."

"That says a whole lot, then." Stan turned to go into the house. "I'll try to hold back the stampede when you come in."

Craig thanked him then texted Pat. *I'm a bit disappointed you didn't invite me to join your 'hot date.'* Leering emoji. *Dinner sounds lovely though. Can you meet me at the BBQ place in Pipe Creek at 5:00 or should I pick you up?*

An embarrassed emoji followed by *I'll be there* was her response.

He couldn't seem to wipe the goofy grin off his face no matter how he tried, so Craig took the scenic route back inside—around the house—where he found the girls playing horseshoes, and the boys throwing a football, in the yard. He watched for a minute, caught a stray pass. Tossing the ball back to Richard, he went through the kitchen, and into the living room, where everyone lounged around the television. "Ace, Amber, can I speak to you? In the den. Alone."

He walked down the hall, into the den, and waited.

"Something wrong?" His son asked.

Craig shook his head. "I...uh..." He cleared his throat. Swallowed hard. Took a deep breath and fumbled through the announcement that he'd met someone.

"Is it the lady from the club the other night?" The excitement on his daughter's face, and in her voice, made him wince.

"Yes. As I said then, I ran into her at Harry's old place. She thought I was Scott. We've visited a time or two since."

"How does she know Scott?"

"They worked together thirty-something years ago. She'd seen me, and Robert, in town a week or so before, and we reminded her of him."

"Oh... Wow..."

Craig could almost see his daughter's romantic heart take flight, hear the wheels of her imagination turn. He sighed. "Anyway, we're having dinner Saturday, and I want you, just the two of you, to come and meet her."

"Why just us?" Ace asked.

"Because I'd like for her to get to know you two, before I throw her into the fray of a Sunday dinner with the whole bunch. Stanley met her the other day..." Craig realized his faux pas when surprised shock filled Amber's eyes. "Now, don't go in there and get on his case, Amber. I practically begged him not to say anything."

"You asked my husband to lie to me?" Fury laced her tone.

"No." Craig's voice was firm. "I asked him to respect my privacy until I could tell you myself."

"And you've waited.... How long?"

"Three whole days, Amber."

"You just said you've visited with her a time or two

since steak night. That's over a week ago. Not three days."

Craig ground his teeth. The muscle in his jaw twitched. A dead giveaway he was reaching the end of his patience. Ace stepped up, cut off his response, and calmed his sister's wrath, with a stroke on her arm.

"Stan's right. Daddy has a right to his privacy, and we have to respect that. Or at least try to understand."

Which convinced Craig his son didn't understand in the least, considering they talked, alone, nearly every night. *They'll just have to deal with it.* "So, will you meet me?"

"Sure, we will, Dad. What time?"

He'd asked Pat to meet him at five, so he told them to get there around seven. How they got through the rest of the afternoon without a major blowup would puzzle him forever. Thankfully, after dessert, everyone loaded up leftovers and went home. Goodbyes from his daughter and son-in-law were a bit strained.

* * *

From the tension in his wife's posture, Stan wondered how big of a tongue-lashing he was in for. Thankfully, their three children were spread out among the other family members' houses. He and Amber could hash it all out and be done. She waited until they arrived home before addressing the issue uppermost in their minds.

"I know Daddy asked you not to, but I'm still trying to understand why you didn't tell me you'd met this woman. We've never kept secrets from each other."

"No. We haven't, and I don't plan to start. But, you know how challenging it can be when loyalty is tested, in a situation that could cause tension between those you love."

"I just don't get it. Why would he feel the need to keep her a secret? It's not like we haven't been after him, for years, to get out more and be open to meeting someone."

"Exactly. You, and Ace, have been so concerned over his lack of motivation to do that, he probably didn't want to get your hopes up. You should have seen your face, when you told Trina he'd met someone, and that you were meeting her Saturday night. This has got to be a huge adjustment for him, Amber. He and your mother were married so long, and she's been gone for over a decade. Give him some slack."

"I just want him to be happy, truly happy, again."

"As I've said before, numerous times, he has to get there in his own way, and in his own time."

Amber rolled her eyes. "So, what did you think about her?"

"First impression?"

She nodded.

"She's an attractive lady. She seemed a bit shy. Definitely as surprised as your dad was when I showed up." He chuckled. "You should have seen him fumble through the introduction. Then, when he implied I shouldn't say anything, she stormed off, and slammed into the truck."

"Really?"

"Yeah. He's probably over the moon that she's still talking to him."

"I'm sure she knows a good man when she meets one."

Stan grinned and slid his arms around her waist. "Do you?"

She leaned into him. "Yes. I do. Knew it the moment our eyes met on that homecoming eve so long ago."

Grateful the conversation went smoother than he'd imagined, Stanley swept her into his arms and carried her to their bed.

Chapter Thirteen

Pat transferred the last load of sheets from one machine to the other, then folded the hamper of towels she'd removed from the dryer. Between yesterday afternoon and now, she, Marcey, and Missy had cleaned and restocked the empty cabins, scrubbed the kitchen, and froze or repurposed Thanksgiving leftovers. She'd enjoyed her hour in the sauna and another in the whirlpool. As soon as she finished this chore, she'd be out of here and on her way to get ready for dinner with Craig. Never in her wildest dreams had she imagined missing one person so much.

Anne stepped through the laundry room door. "There you are. I've been all over looking for you."

Pat laughed. "You know me, can't stay still when there are things to be done."

"Can't thank you enough for helping this week." She reached over and slid a check into Pat's shirt pocket. "Hopefully, this will express our gratitude. Somewhat."

"I'm sure it's more than plenty."

"We're taking the crew out for our usual employee appreciation dinner. I hope you'll join us."

"Thanks, but I already have dinner plans."

Surprise registered on Anne's face. Curiosity lit her gaze. "Someone special?"

Warmth filled Pat's heart. Infused her cheeks. "Could be. I think. Time will tell, I guess."

"You're welcome to invite him, or her, to dinner with us."

Since they'd never spoken of her love life, Pat understood Anne's comment. Particularly in light of the times they lived in. She smiled. "Him. And had I known this yesterday, we'd be there. But our plans are already set. Maybe some other time. Thanks, though."

Anne hugged her. "I know you're heading back to Mississippi soon. Give my cousin and his lovely bride a hug from us and tell them to hurry back. And to bring you with them when they come."

"Will do."

Thirty minutes later, Pat drove through the Crossed Penn's gate. She arrived at Garrett's cabin in less than half an hour. She poured herself the last glass of wine, from the bottle she and Craig shared a week ago and plopped down on the couch. Propping her feet on the tiny coffee table, she sipped the sweet, red liquid and debated what to wear tonight. They were having bar-b-que, so fancy wasn't necessary. But she'd love to dress up for a change. Especially after the week of grunge and grease she'd worn.

Closing her eyes, she asked for guidance in her choice of clothing and allowed her mind to empty. The image of a cashmere sweater she hadn't donned in a long time, flashed through her head. Paired with fur-lined boots, nice jeans and accessories should more than suffice. She finished her wine, showered, and dressed. She was never one for much makeup, so she dabbed a bit of color on her eyelids, darkened her lashes with a touch of mascara and swiped on lip gloss. Standing before the full-length mirror, she appraised the woman staring back at her.

Longer than she'd worn it in years, her hair needed a trim. *Who knows, maybe I'll let it grow out for once.* Slender waist, slight curve of hip, small but still firm breasts. *Not bad for a woman flirting with sixty.*

Not that she'd ever really cared. Oh, she'd gone to great lengths to maintain her health. Eating reasonably clean. Most of the time. Daily/weekly exercise for cardio, strength, and agility. Ample time for R&R to keep the energy high, and life—mind, body, and soul—in balance. But she'd always believed a woman did not need to enhance or change what nature gave her to impress a man. Or anyone else, for that matter. What you see is what you get. Like it? Good. No? Your loss. Don't need that kind of negativity in my life.

Craig sure seems to like it.

She glanced at the clock, and her stomach lurched in a moment of panic that she'd be late. She grabbed a jacket on her way out the door.

Time's an illusion, she reminded herself on the drive to Pipe Creek. She arrived at the restaurant to find Craig, pacing the parking lot. His grin and the quick flash of relief in his eyes sent her heart into a tailspin. He opened her door before she could even unbuckle her seat belt. "Sorry, I'm late."

He glanced at his watch. "You're not. I'm early."

He held a hand toward her. Pat placed her palm in his, allowing him to pull her from the car and into his arms. They embraced for a long moment. Words weren't necessary, but he voiced them anyway. "I missed you."

She squeezed him tight and skimmed her lips across his cheek. "The ranch was a madhouse this week. It's a wonder I had time to think." Smile. Wink. "But I managed to miss you too."

He grinned. "Good. Hungry?"

She nodded. "Starved."

"Let's go, then."

Within minutes, they were seated at a table, given glasses of water and menus. Once food and drinks were ordered, he took her hand in his. Played with the wrist and caressed the palm in a way that had her senses buzzing. Pat stopped the sensuous torture by taking a sip of water. "How was your week?"

"Interesting. Had a close call with a ceiling beam so decided I'm not going to attempt repairs or remodeling. Tore the whole thing down."

"Wow." She placed her hands in her lap, relieved when the waiter brought their salads.

"Yep. Going to rebuild according to the original structure with the additions I'd planned."

Craig made quick work of the salad while she couldn't get a single piece of lettuce past her tight throat. She drank more water, then picked out a cherry tomato, relished the juicy taste of it, and forked up another bite. "Sounds nice. And how was your day, yesterday?"

"Great. Did you get a chance to relax much at all? Other than your whirlpool and sauna. Pretty mean of you to mention that, by the way, without issuing an invitation."

Pat nearly choked on her spring greens. Heat flamed her face, but she didn't dare comment. He reached out to caress her cheek with the back of his hand. A low chuckle sounded in his throat. Suddenly, afraid of the intensity of his gaze, and the crazy way her heart flip-flopped at the slightest touch, she leaned back, patted her lips with the napkin, and sighed with relief when the waiter appeared with the rest of their meals. "We pushed to finish up yesterday and this morning. But it's all done. In fact, think I'll go home earlier than I planned."

Disappointment flashed across his features. "Not too soon, I hope. Thought we could spend the day together tomorrow."

"Don't you have family obligations tomorrow?"

"Not this weekend. The kids will be getting their children ready for school on Monday. Speaking of..."

She waited while he cut his steak. Took a bite of her own. Surprised pleasure hummed through her when the tender meat practically melted on her tongue. "Speaking of...?"

"I hope you don't mind, but I asked my two to join us afterwhile."

She winced inwardly. "Uh..."

Craig put his fork and knife down and unsnapped his phone from its holster. "I guess I should have asked you first. Sorry. But we'd talked about you meeting them next week, so thought I'd get a jump on that."

Pat stopped him from calling them. "No. It's fine. I'm surprised, is all."

"You sure? I can cancel. They're not due here until seven."

Pat looked over his shoulder at the clatter of boots on the hardwood floor accompanied by a low, feminine laugh. "Looks like they're early."

Craig shoved back from the table and turned. "Hey, you guys. I thought we'd agreed on seven?"

His daughter slid her arm through his. "You always told us, if we're not at least fifteen minutes early, we're late. Besides, you said *around* seven."

The tease in her tone could not be mistaken, nor was it missed by either Pat or Craig. He glanced at his watch, gave her a pointed look, and shook his head with a resigned sigh.

Pat rose when he held a hand toward her. "Pat Greene, my daughter, Amber, and son…"

Before Craig could finish, his son stepped forward, tipped his hat, and introduced himself. "Ace Harris, ma'am. Pleased to meet you. Looks like we interrupted y'all's meal. Sorry 'bout that."

She sent Craig an inquisitive look. "I'm curious as to *why* you'd name your son, Ace?"

The three of them snickered. Ace removed his hat, offered her his hand. "Short for Adam Craig Harris the fourth, ma'am."

Charmed by the younger version of Craig, with those same laughing gray eyes and cocky grin, Pat accepted his handshake without hesitation. She nodded at the girl. "Nice to meet you both. Have a seat."

"Have y'all had dinner?" Craig asked, after everyone sat.

"Oh yeah. We'll be eating the remaining ham, and turkey, for days," Ace admitted with a chuckle. "How 'bout you, Miss Pat? How was your Thanksgiving?"

Craig's wink set her at ease. "Pat worked through Thanksgiving, at the Crossed Penn ranch, in Utopia."

"Really?" The two asked in unison.

Pat nodded. "Temporary fill-in, to help out friends."

Much like with their father, conversation flowed, smooth as silk, among the four of them. Pat loved the way both kids interacted with Craig. They way they laughed and joked warmed her heart in the same manner time spent with Melena's family did. Too soon, the waiter appeared to remove their plates and offer dessert, which

Amber, and Ace, partook in. Afterward, the two got up to leave. The warmth of Amber's gaze, and the absolute adoration on Craig's face, when she whispered something to him, and he hugged her, put to rest any fears Pat might have had about the impression she made.

"Your children are great," she said, as Craig helped her into her jacket, after he'd paid the tab.

He stroked his hands down her arms. "Thanks. Get that from their mother."

She turned and cupped his cheek in her palm. "Oh, I'm sure there's quite a bit of you in there somewhere."

He scoffed and shrugged into his coat. "Yeah. The impatience. Fifteen minutes early, my foot."

They walked to her car in companionable silence. "Wish you were still at the hotel."

The image his words conjured sent delicious shivers along every nerve ending in her body. Still, she sent him a questioning look. "Oh?"

Ruddy color infused his face, as the implication of how his remark sounded, sank in. He cleared his throat. "Then I wouldn't have to worry about you driving so far."

Laughter rang out in the evening air, as they said goodnight, and vowed to call one another once each arrived home safely.

Chapter Fourteen

Stan met them at the door when Ace dropped Amber off. "Well?"

Amber's smile had a wistful bent to it.

"She's lovely. He lights up when he looks at her." Her lips quivered. A tear trembled on her lashes. "Like the way he used to look at Mama."

Ace confirmed his sister's statement with a nod. "I liked her on the spot."

"Yeah, there's something so... real...so... honest, and authentic about her. She's got the most beautiful eyes. Deep blue. Almost violet."

Stan's relief escaped in an exhale. "Good. Now maybe we can let him be and allow him to do this *his* way."

Both looked at him like he'd lost his mind.

All three laughed.

"I bet Mama, and Scott, are up there orchestrating this whole thing."

The air shifted and vibrated around them at Ace's statement.

Amber's eyes glazed over in wonderment. "That'd be just like 'em."

Stan chuckled. "All right, miss romance author. Don't go there right now. You'll be awake all night."

Ace kissed his sister's cheek and bid them goodbye.

Stanley urged his wife into bed, where he did his best to empty her mind of any thoughts but his love for her.

* * *

Craig barely made it out of the restaurant parking lot when he had the urge to hear her voice. Engaging his hands-free phone feature, he called Pat.

"Hello?"

"I'm not ready for this night to end. Are you too tired to grab a drink and perhaps a dance or two?"

She hesitated. "Honestly? Yes. But I really appreciate the offer, Cowboy. Sleep tight and we'll talk in the morning."

"OK. Drive safe."

"You, too."

He disconnected and turned the truck toward the Rockin' H. He arrived to find Ace sitting on the porch, feet propped on the rail, a glass of brandy in his hand.

"Have a shot with me, Dad?"

"Love one." Craig toed off his boots and took the chair next to his son. They listened to the sound of night critters around them.

"Ms. Pat make it home?"

"Haven't heard yet. I'm sure she'll let me know. Although I might not get the message until later with the patchy service in that area." He sipped. *Hope he doesn't want to engage in a drawn-out conversation.* More like an interrogation.

As though Ace had read his mind, he leaned forward, picked up the bottle and refreshed their drinks. "I'm not going to ask you a bunch of questions, Dad. I realize you two just met. I will say Amber, and I, both like her. But... Be careful. Get to know her before you put your heart on the line."

Too late for that. "Thanks, Ace."

Ace clinked his glass against Craig's. "Anytime. Love you, Dad."

"Love you too, Son."

He stayed on the porch long after Ace retired. When Pat's message came in that she had arrived home safely, he went upstairs and changed into pajamas. Propping against the headboard, he scrolled through his recent call list, and hit redial.

"Hey."

That heart his son didn't want him to put on the line tremored. "Wanted your voice to be the last thing I heard before going to sleep."

"'Night, Cowboy. Sweet dreams."

"You'll be in them so I'm sure they will be. Dream of me," he whispered.

* * *

Craig awoke, drained from dreams that weren't so sweet. He'd tossed and turned, seeking rest from the constant flow of vignettes of his and Tamera's life, her death, and being enveloped in a deep, dark pit. Pat appeared in some, running toward him. Running away. On occasion, he'd be within arm's length, and she'd walk right through him into Scott's embrace. Frustrated at what all this might mean, he stumbled out of bed, and into the shower, hoping the hot water would ease the chill lingering in the wake of a night of misery.

"Just dreams, Craig," he told himself. Random fears brought on from the excitement and nerves of the last few days. Feeling better, he dried off and wrapped a towel around his waist. He picked his phone up off the bedside table, sat and called. *Please be awake.*

The connection was so bad when she answered all he heard was *later... emergency... Crossed Penn.*

Fear clutched his chest. His fingers shook while he searched through his contacts. Finding Mike's number, he hit the send button, put the phone on speaker, and set it down while he dressed. "Hey, buddy. There's an emergency at the Crossed Penn ranch in Utopia. You want to ride out there with me to see what's going on?"

Mike said he'd be ready by the time Craig got there.

* * *

Pat awoke worn out from a night fraught with wild imaginings that made no sense to her rational brain.... She and Craig, living happily ever after. Herself, him, or Scott, weeping in a cemetery. Melena and her children gathered around a freshly dug grave. *Oh, God, not again!* she'd think, then Garrett would appear, and all would be well. Her feet hadn't hit the floor when Anne Penn called. "Hey, Anne, what's up?"

"Missy is having stomach cramps and some light bleeding. Think you..."

Pat interrupted that she'd be right there and lunged from beneath the covers. In record time, she dressed, prepared herself a travel mug of coffee, and headed to the Crossed Penn. Craig's call came through during the drive. "Have to call you later. Missy's in trouble. I'm on my way to the Crossed Penn. I'll let you know if she's OK, or we're taking her to the nearest emergency room."

She drove through the gate and to the bunkhouse where Brock—white as a ghost—and Kidd, paced the porch.

"Anne and Marcey are with her. They drove me out."

Pat took a moment to run a soothing hand down his arm. "I'm sure she'll be fine. We'll let you know ASAP."

She entered the home and went straight to the bedroom. "What's happening?"

Missy groaned. Her face twisted with pain. "My stomach hurts."

"OK." Pat sat beside her and swiped a hand across her forehead. "No fever. Stretch out, honey."

"I can't."

Panic filled the room. Tense. Wary. Tangible. Pat sucked in a breath, exhaled slowly, and tuned in to her intuition. Anne lit some herbs, opened the window, and began to chant prayers in her Native American tongue.

"What's that smell?" Missy asked.

"Sage."

"That's to run off evil spirits, right?" Marcey asked.

As a young mother who'd had her share of pregnancy scares, she should know better. Pat bit back the retort that sprang to her tongue. "No. It's to clear out negative energy brought on by fear. There are no evil spirits here. Marcey, would you mind preparing her a cup of peppermint tea? I think there's some in the lodge."

Marcey nodded and went to do as asked. Half of the tension in the room went along with her. Pat sighed with relief. "I want you to look at me, Missy."

The girl's terrified gaze met hers. Pat smiled. "Take a deep breath. Slow and easy. Four counts on the inhale, six on exhale."

She coached her through a couple, then encouraged her to stretch out so she could examine her. Missy did as requested tension evident in her every move.

"Good. Now, I want you to try and relax. Continue with the slow breaths." Pat pressed gently on Missy's abdomen while she questioned her. "What did you eat for supper last night?"

"Jalapeño poppers and fajita's."

"You might want to lay off those for a while," Pat said with a chuckle. "Did you pick up on anything heavy or strain in any way?"

Missy shook her head.

"Good." Pat checked her blood pressure, pulse, and heart rate, which were all slightly elevated. *Probably due to anxiety.* "Did you and Brock make love last night or this morning?"

Missy turned beet red and nodded.

"That's OK. It's perfectly fine to do so, but you might abstain for a week or two. When is your next doctor's appointment."

"A couple weeks, I think. I have it on my calendar."

"Ok. How heavy is the bleeding? Light, moderate, flowing?"

"Only a few spots."

"That's a good sign. How are you feeling now?"

"Better," Missy replied, her relief palpable.

"OK. I'm pretty sure what you're experiencing is a result of the food you consumed and the sexual activity. Could be hormones or something equally non-threatening. But panicking is the worst thing you can do. Do you understand?"

Tears welled in the young girl's eyes. Her lips trembled. "I don't want to lose my baby."

"I understand that. So, from now on, when

something causes you fear, I want you to learn to meditate for a few minutes, or something, to calm yourself before you panic."

"I've never meditated before."

Pat helped her sit up and stroked a hand down her cheek. "You just did. Those deep breaths while quieting your mind is a form of meditation. You might also repeat a mantra."

"What is that?"

"A prayer or positive statement. Something like, 'my baby is healthy.' Or 'my baby is divinely protected.' In fact, it wouldn't hurt for you to make a conscious effort to keep those statements running through your mind at all times."

"Brock and I are Catholic. We've been praying to the Holy Mother and St. Gerard Majella—the patron saint of expectant mothers."

"See, divinely protected," Anne said, speaking for the first time since the ordeal began. "All types, and every form, of prayer are powerful *if* the faith you put behind them is true and deep. But your ultimate trust should be in the intelligent love, the goodness, and the sovereignty of the Creator. There is a divine purpose behind whatever happens. Even if the outcome is different than what you're praying for."

Pat's heart did a happy little flip at the light in Missy's eyes. "Thank you, Miss Pat. You too, Mrs. Anne."

Pat hugged her. "Anytime, sweetheart. I want you to stay in bed today and keep your feet propped up. Let Brock pamper you. We'll check on you throughout the day."

Missy giggled.

Marcey walked in with the tea. "There's a gentleman here to see you, and he brought a doctor with him."

Chapter Fifteen

A young woman about Amber's age, met Craig, and Mike, in the lodge.

"May I help you?"

"Looking for Pat Greene. Heard there was an emergency out here. This is Dr. Guidry." Craig pointed to Mike.

"Miss Pat, and Mrs. Anne, are out at the bunkhouse with Missy. You can follow me if you'd like. I'm Marcey."

"Thanks, Marcey."

"What'cha got there?" Mike asked.

"Peppermint tea. Miss Pat said it would help Missy."

Mike acknowledged her comment with a noncommittal hum.

The two men walked with her toward a mobile home behind the lodge, and waited on the porch with Marcey's husband, and the father-to-be. Craig had made his third trek across the deck when the door opened, and Pat walked out. The swift surge of joy he felt at seeing her, dimmed somewhat by the confusion in her expression.

"Craig?"

"Hey, I brought Mike out in case he could be of service."

"I told you I'd call if we had to go to the ER or something."

Craig shook his head. "All I heard was 'later,' 'emergency,' and 'Crossed Penn.'"

Pat rolled her eyes, cursed the cell service, and shook Mike's hand. "Nice to meet you, Dr. Guidry. Missy's fine."

"I'd be happy to check her out if you think it's

necessary."

Brock spoke up that he'd feel better. "Not that I don't trust you, Miss Pat…"

Pat smiled to ease the fear and consternation on his face. "I understand, Brock. I'll go check with Missy."

Within moments, she returned to escort Mike into the house. "Brock, you can come with us if you'd like." She looked at Craig. "Sorry, but you'll have to wait here. Or in the lodge if that's more comfortable."

Craig leaned a hip against the railing, and tucked his hands into his jacket pockets, to stop himself from reaching for her. "This is fine."

Kidd excused himself to go tend to the horses.

Marcey came out and chatted with him about everything except the questions burning in her gaze. Had Pat mentioned him to any of them? Why not, considering the scene she'd made about not being his dirty little secret?

She came out of the house and walked over to him. "Thank you, for coming to the rescue."

Her smile, the warmth in her tone, and the light in those expressive eyes, nearly brought him to his knees. Craig put both hands on her waist and drew her close. "Anytime."

Something about the tension in her stance stopped his kiss.

"Anne will be out in a minute. She's invited you and Mike to stay for breakfast."

"That sounds nice."

Conversation halted when a small woman of Native American heritage, and Mike, walked through the door.

Pat turned and extended a hand to introduce them.

"Craig, meet Anne Penn, a dear friend and owner of the Crossed Penn. Anne, this is Craig Harris..."

"Of the Rockin' H' ranch." Anne smiled and held a hand out to him.

Craig accepted the shake with one hand, tipped his hat with the other. "Nice to meet you, ma'am."

"My husband, Bill, should have breakfast ready soon. You two are staying. Aren't you?"

"Unless Mike has reason not to."

Mike shook his head.

Craig grinned. "We'd be delighted. Thank you."

"Great," Anne said, and slipped her arm through Mike's. "Marcey, will you please come with me? We'll need to prepare a tray for the expectant parents. Missy is to stay off her feet today."

The three walked away, leaving Craig, and Pat, alone. "I hope I didn't overstep any boundaries. You seemed a bit... surprised, maybe a little putout, that we're here."

She stepped into his embrace. "Put out? Not at all. Surprised, yes. Could have saved you, and Mike, a trip if you'd called."

"Didn't think about that. Besides, then I couldn't have done this..." He lowered his voice. Nudged her nose with his. Brushed a tiny kiss across her mouth. "Good morning, beautiful."

She melted against him. Allowed a deeper kiss and whispered, "'Morning, Cowboy," against his lips.

The breakfast bell interrupted further intimacy. Craig's stomach clenched like a nervous fist at the joy on Mike's face, when he, and Pat, entered the lodge hand-in-hand.

"How long have you been a nurse?" Mike asked, once they were seated, plates piled high with eggs, bacon, biscuits, and gravy.

"I've been an RN for thirty years, NP twenty-something, and an Energy Medicine Practitioner going on ten."

"Really? I find Energy Medicine so fascinating."

"Here we go." Craig's chuckle cut off the animated discussion about to take place and brought a round of laughter.

Mike leaned back in his chair. "We'll have to get together and chat sometime. But not today." He scooted away from the table, stood, put his dishes in the bin, and addressed Craig. "You about ready?"

Anne must have sensed his hesitancy because she hurried to stem his response. "No need to rush. Y'all are welcome to stay a while."

Mike gave Craig a pointed look. "I promised Rikki Jayne we'd go on a ride today."

"Wonderful!" Anne gushed. "Bring your family out. We'll take them on a trail ride and have dinner together. Yours too, Craig."

Craig appreciated the effort but wasn't sure he wanted to share Pat with the entire Harris/Hensley clan so soon. Having her meet his children, and Mike, was enough for now. He gathered her plate, along with his, and carried them to the bin. She finished her juice and brought the glass to him. "Dinner tonight?"

"Dinner sounds lovely."

"I'll call you, and we'll hash out the details later."

She acknowledged him with a smile and nod.

They bid everyone goodbye and accepted thanks—

again—and left.

"So...?"

Craig chortled. "So, I'll save you the trouble of prying. I met her a couple of weeks ago. She thought I was Scott. Seems she was working the same medical mission trip as he, when his parents, and first wife, were killed, thirty-something years ago. We've spent time together, since. Ace, and Amber, met her last night. Despite my son's warning, I've found myself captivated sooner than reasonable or sensible."

Mike's hand on his shoulder conveyed both compassion and encouragement. "There are some things the heart knows that the mind can't explain."

Chapter Sixteen

Pat checked on Missy once more then left the Crossed Penn. Once ensconced in Garrett's cabin, she allowed the many emotions she'd suppressed, to flow through, and out, of her. In the first half of her career, *no one,* other than Scott, had shown her the courtesy of confidence in her ability and training. The initial surge of anger, and betrayal, she'd felt upon learning Craig had brought Mike Guidry to the ranch, assured her she still had some healing, and letting go, to do.

Changing into workout clothes, she relaxed into her usual morning routine. While in deep contemplation, she allowed all the doubt, insecurity, and frustration, she'd experienced as a young nurse to come up. Surrendering into the sensations, she prayed and asked the Holy Spirit's help to alchemize them into wisdom. Hopefully, she would be able to assist someone else in processing the same or familiar feelings. Afterward, she showered, dressed, and checked her messages for the third time in as many hours. *Now what?*

She hadn't heard from Craig. Anne's latest message indicated Missy was already getting impatient being in bed. She walked around the cabin, picking up here... Rearranging there... Cleaning this... Organizing that. Homesickness washed over her in waves. She removed her luggage from the closet and started packing. By the time she'd set her last item of clothing in the case, and began loading her overnight bag, she'd decided to leave for Mississippi. *You agreed to have dinner with Craig.*

He'll understand. And if he didn't.... Pat shrugged. Then maybe they weren't meant to be together.

She set the bags by the door and prepared to text him when a knock rapped against the wooden barrier. She opened it, and there he stood, holding a bouquet of flowers so huge he needed both hands. No man had *ever* given her flowers!

Love swarmed through her. Tears filled her eyes. Clogged her throat. Rolled down her cheeks. She practically dragged him into the cabin. Once he set the vase down, she jumped into his arms, raining kisses over his entire face.

Laughter rumbled in his chest. He set her on her feet and enveloped her in an embrace so fierce, a kiss so consuming, it left her weak, and trembling, against his hard body. He picked her up, carried her to the couch, and settled with her cuddled against his chest.

"Dang, had I known I'd get this kind of response, I'd have brought flowers every time I saw you." His hands ran over her back in a restless caress. Those expressive gray eyes turned smokey. Pat snuggled, resting her head on his shoulder, until the tension passed.

She peeked over his shoulder. The bouquet was actually a hodgepodge of different flowers, shoved into the largest vase she'd ever seen. Probably the largest he could find on a Sunday. Didn't matter, they were *beautiful*.

His charming grin, followed by a chuckle, danced along her spine. "I couldn't get rid of Mike and back here soon enough. Had to go to Boerne for the flowers. No florists are open today, so I did the best I could."

"They're perfect. Thank you," she whispered against his lips. "Would you like a cup of coffee or something to drink?"

Craig tightened his arms. "Then I'd have to let you up."

She sighed. "Can't sit like this all day. Your legs'll go numb."

He shifted, stretched. "I'll take my chances."

Pat laughed, hugged him again, climbed off his lap, and held her hand out for him to hold while they walked the short distance into the kitchen. "Coffee? Tea?"

"Coffee's fine." He stopped mid-stride. "You're packed already?"

She nodded. "Figured I'd get an early start."

"I thought we were having dinner."

Her previous thoughts of leaving today dissipated like whisps of fog in the chilly air. She stood on tiptoe and pressed her lips against his cheek. "We are."

"I wish you'd stay. Leave on Wednesday like you originally planned."

She moved forward a couple of steps, gathered cups, and poured. Handed him one. "I've nothing to do until Wednesday. Besides, aren't you going to start building a new home?"

He winced. "Yeah, but I can put that off until next week while you're gone. Or at least until Thursday."

Pat shook her head, sipped, and smiled to herself at how easily he'd consider changing his plans for her. Another first. "How about we take a drive to Lost Maples?"

Craig put their cups in the sink and ran water in them. "Not really dressed for a hike."

"Me either. But a walk would be nice. Plenty of trails don't require climbing gear."

"Let's do it."

Pat marveled at the beauty of the big-tooth Maple trees, and other foliage, along the drive leading to a short trail. Craig stayed close beside, or behind her, except to help her cross a creek, or step over fallen trees or rotten logs. They stopped at a lookout point where earth and sky melded in a glorious profusion of light and color. Craig slid his arms around her waist and rested his cheek against her head.

"It's so beautiful here."

He hummed his agreement. "Would you consider staying here? With me? Permanently."

Pat's heart plummeted at the thought that all he might want from her was a live-in lover. She tried to hide her disappointment with a tiny laugh. "I think the Texas Forest Service might have something to say about that."

His chortle reverberated through her. "I didn't mean here, literally."

"I'm ready to go home, Craig. Melena, and Garrett, will be in, Thursday. The family get-together is on Saturday. Besides, it's kinda soon for us to be considering that, isn't it?"

He turned her in his embrace. Cupped her face in his hands. "I didn't ask for an answer. Yet. Only that you mull over the possibility. You've still got a whole lot of Harris/Hensley clan to meet. After which, you're liable to run off screaming, never to be found in Bandera again," he warned with a chuckle.

She snickered. "I don't scare easily, Cowboy."

They stayed in the park for hours, walking, sharing patches of conversation interspersed with long stretches of companionable silence. As darkness descended, they drove into Hondo for dinner. Craig dropped her back at the cabin around nine then texted an hour later that he'd safely made it to the Rockin' H.

* * *

Pat drove out to the Crossed Penn to check on Missy, who was up and about early. She returned Garrett's key to Anne, and then got on the road. She spent the night in Louisiana and arrived in her Mississippi hometown Tuesday afternoon. She'd always loved the little house she'd grown up in, and maintained ownership of, after her parents passed away. But now, it seemed so big. So empty.

Thursday morning, Melena called the moment their plane touched down on American soil. Pat answered, "Hey, friend."

"Where are you?"

"I'm home. How long before y'all fly into Baton Rouge?"

"We have a two-hour layover. We'll arrive at BR Metro around four o'clock. Should be home by six or seven."

"Y'all aren't spending the night?"

"Nah, we're ready to be in our own bed."

"OK. Keep me posted on your trip. Can't wait to see you both and get all the details."

"Me too." A click interrupted further conversation. "That's Kathryn. I'll talk to you later."

"K. Bye." Pat barely had time to end the call before her phone rang again. Craig. "Hey, Cowboy. How's it going?"

"Be much better if you were here."

The longing in his voice did delicious things to her insides. "I'll be back soon."

"Not soon enough. Hear from your friend... Melena... Right?"

"Yes. Just hung up with her. They'll be home later this afternoon."

"Great. Just wanted to hear your voice. Have a good evening, and wonderful visit, then get yourself back here."

"A bit demanding, aren't you?"

She didn't miss the hint of loneliness in his husky tone when he added, "Please."

Chapter Seventeen

Craig slid his phone into its holster. A bit demanding, huh? If he had any sense—and wasn't afraid she'd send him packing with his tail tucked between his legs—he'd drive to Mississippi and drag her back. Kicking and screaming if necessary.

That won't work with Pat any more than it did with Tamera. He laughed inwardly at the thought. Probably not, but oh, to feel like his old self again was more than worth the inclination.

He'd been numb with pain for so long that he doubted he'd ever find that arrogant, cocky cowboy the women in his life loved to hate. Hated to love. *Whatever.* He'd never hoped to feel this young and full of life, full of hope, again.

Whistling, he continued to work. With each nail he hammered into place he finally understood that life was finally worth living again.

He'd finished lunch when Mike approached. "Hey buddy, what's up?"

Mike shrugged. "Thought I'd ride out and check on your progress."

Craig arched a brow at him. "Really?"

Mike had the grace to flush. "That, and to be sure you're OK, since no one can reach you."

"Oh, for heaven's sake." Craig tried to sound disgruntled. He really did. The grin gave him away. "Amber?"

Mike laughed. "Yeah. You'll have to get a landline if you plan on staying out here, much. Otherwise, your daughter will be a nervous wreck."

Craig shook his head. "I have no idea how to reassure her I'm fine."

Mike eyed him for a moment. "Keep on doing what you're doing. She'll ease up, eventually."

Craig considered Mike's comment. Frowned. "You think so?"

Mike moved closer. "There's a light in your eyes I haven't seen in a long time, Craig. None of us have. I reckon Amber will see it soon enough, too."

Guilt at what his prolonged grief put his children through, momentarily clouded the joy in Craig's heart. Mike must have seen something in his expression because he stepped forward and put a hand on his shoulder.

"Don't go beating yourself up, Craig. Grief is a journey. Some of us take longer to reach the end than others. You'll always love Tamera, and part of you will mourn her loss forever. But it's OK to live and to love again."

"I'm realizing that. Finally. Not sure how much is due to meeting Pat or simply coming into it on my own."

"Doesn't matter. It's the progress that counts. So, you think you have a future with Pat?"

"I sure hope so."

"Good. But promise me you won't let it throw you back if that doesn't work out."

Craig grinned. "May not say this often enough, but you're a good friend, Mike. I can see why Scott loved and appreciated you so much. I know he'd be relieved you're here watching after Trina and the kids."

Mike's eyes lit up at that. "Thanks."

* * *

Pat walked with her friend along the track at the city park. Garrett had holed himself up in the studio. Melena arrived at her house earlier this morning all atwitter. Pat sat through hours of photos and detailed descriptions of where they'd been, what they'd seen and done, and who they'd met. She sensed a host of unanswered questions and curiosity beneath Melena's excitement. When she ran out of breath, Melena urged Pat down beside her on a bench, and asked for an update on her, and Craig's, relationship, insisting on getting all the details.

"I hardly know where to start."

Melena hugged her. "Last time we talked for more than a few minutes, you cooked dinner for him."

Pat filled her in on what had happened since. How wonderful that Saturday was. The fight they had on Monday, and how crazy Thanksgiving week at the ranch had been. She told her about meeting Craig's son, and daughter, and how beautifully the three interacted. And, of him bringing Mike out to the Crossed Penn to check on Missy. "He is so much like Scott, and yet, not. Like one of those pictures that appear to be something else depending on the angle from which it is observed. It's downright scary sometimes."

"But you like him, don't you? Really like him."

"When he brought those flowers, which I still have, by the way, I fell completely head over heels."

"And that's what scares you the most."

"Yeah. Seems like it should be too soon to be so in love. So... connected."

"Was it the same with Scott? The instant

connection? I know I felt that way about Garrett, and Jon had only been gone seven months."

Pat nodded. "Pretty much."

Melena squealed. "Oh, I am so excited for you!"

"Calm down. We're a long way from happy ever after."

"Maybe so, but you can't stop love. I can't believe the Crossed Penn crew got to meet him before I did."

Pat chortled. "You'll have to take that up with Craig."

* * *

Get-togethers with Melena's family had always filled Pat's heart to overflowing. But this time, she arrived home afterward, with an ache in her chest. She washed her face, put on pajamas, and barely settled into bed when the phone rang. *Melena.* "Hello?"

"Are you OK?"

Tears welled in Pat's eyes. She swallowed hard. "Yeah. Just...."

"Don't lie to me or try to hide your feelings. You miss him, don't you?"

Pat inhaled a deep, shuddering breath. "Yes. I miss him. More than I thought possible. More than I should."

"There's no 'should' when you love someone. Tell him. Don't let this chance pass you by."

"Wish it were that easy."

"It can be. Go back to Bandera. The cabin is yours until we come after Christmas. I know, since your parents died, you usually celebrate with us. But we'll understand if you stay there this year."

"I'll think about it."

"No, don't. I'm going to tell you like you told me. Follow your heart without overthinking the idea or worrying it to death."

"But what if he's changed his mind about me? What if he's decided it's just too scary and goes back into his shell?"

"Only one way to find out."

Her phone stuttered, signaling another incoming call. Pat glanced at the screen. "That's him. I'll talk to you later."

She switched over before Melena could respond. "Hey, Cowboy."

"You on your way back yet?"

She giggled. "No."

"Should I hop a plane and come get you?"

The hint of seriousness, underscoring the tease in his voice, eased the ache in Pat's heart. "Melena and I were discussing my return trip to Bandera."

"So, when will you be here?"

"I need a few more days to take care of some things around here. I'll let you know."

"Good. Make it quick."

They talked long into the night until she fell asleep to the sound of his voice.

Chapter Eighteen

This is crazy, Pat thought, as she loaded the suitcase she'd barely unpacked, into the car. *You hardly know the man. And yet...*

She did know him. *He's what you've waited for your entire life.*

How can that be? Is the deep, abiding love she'd dreamed of that simple? That easy?

Last night, when she'd talked to Craig, and voiced her dilemma over Christmas with Melena's family, he provided the perfect solution.

"Fly back to Mississippi for the holiday, and ride with Melena, and Garrett, afterward. That way, you'll have your car here, and can stay as long as you want once they go home."

She still had no idea what she'd do about her job after the first of the year. But for now, she was going to Bandera and, hopefully, to a future with the man she loved with every fiber of her being.

Crazy.

Melena arrived to see her off.

"Please tell me I'm not losing, haven't lost, my mind."

Melena laughed and hugged her. "Oh, yes. That's exactly what's happened and it's the best thing for you. Let go and enjoy the ride. Keep me posted on your trip."

One last hug and she left her best friend waving in the rearview mirror.

** * **

Craig knew exactly what he wanted. He wanted her in his life. In his arms. In his bed.

He wanted to dream with her at night and wake with her in the mornings.

He wanted what he had with Tamera. Only this time, he'd be wiser, and more insistent, if he felt his love was ignoring her health.

Tamera's voice rose in his mind. *She's not me, Craig. Don't get all clingy and overprotective with this one. She won't tolerate it. She's been independent her entire life. Much more than I was.*

Temper... You're asking me to change who I am.

No. I'm asking you to expand who you are. You are a loving, generous man. Open your mind. Your heart. Life and love are so much more than what we allowed ourselves to believe, or to experience. She can teach you those things. Let go of doubt and fear. Live and love fully—more fully than you've ever dreamed possible, my arrogant jerk Cowboy.

He heard her laughter in his head. Felt her love in his heart. All too soon, her essence faded. *Help me...* Her strength flowed through him from head to toe.

Forgoing the work he'd planned for the afternoon, Craig prepared for Pat's arrival. She'd left Mississippi yesterday, and they'd agreed to meet for a late lunch/early dinner when she got into Bandera, this afternoon. He called Anne Penn to elicit her help, thrilled to find she had a spare key to Garrett's cabin. Meeting her there, Craig had dozens of roses, every color, shape, and size, delivered. He called Pat and begged off from their date, telling her he had an issue with the house to take care of. "I'll grab us something to eat and see you at the cabin as soon as humanly possible."

The disappointment in her voice did his heart good, but he was glad she didn't argue.

At his request, Amber had cooked a full-course meal. Roast with rice and gravy, carrots, and potatoes. Homemade rolls. He set everything in the oven to keep warm. Green salad and Lexie's famously delicious banana pudding. *Hope she likes banana pudding.* In case she didn't, he had a pumpkin pie as a backup. Then, he hid his truck—again, thanks to Anne—and settled in to wait.

A couple of hours later, he heard her suitcase thunk onto the porch floor. Her delighted laughter echoed through the door. He opened it with a flourish. "Like those, do you?"

She gasped and flung herself into his arms. "I love them!"

Craig stumbled a little from the force of her greeting and braced himself against the entryway. "Wait'll you see what awaits you inside."

"My suitcase…," she protested when he lifted her off her feet.

"It'll keep a moment."

He carried her into the house and set her down amongst the virtual garden of flowers gracing the entire cabin.

She began to weep. He cuddled her against his chest. "Oh, Lord, I hope those are happy tears and not allergies."

She giggled and punched him lightly on the arm. "Of course, they're happy tears, you crazy man."

He cradled her face in his hands. "I'll bring you flowers every day for as long as you let me," he whispered between kisses. She wrapped her arms tightly around him and melted. A husky purr reverberated against his lips. Like a bow stretched tight, she began to vibrate in his arms, and nip on the skin showing through the open collar of his shirt. Craig groaned as desire swelled, sharp and painful. He struggled from her grasp. It took every ounce of self-control he possessed, not to pick her up, and carry her into the bedroom. "Whoa. Let's slow down."

He held on when she stiffened in his embrace. Her eyes flashed. Disappointment. Hurt. Anger. Craig shook his head and smoothed his hands down her back in a soothing caress. "Don't look at me like that. I want you. More than the air I breathe. What I don't want, is for this to be something we regret in the morning."

Pleasure replaced the raw emotions in her lovely, violet gaze. "I wouldn't regret a moment I spent with you. But thank you, for thinking I might."

He scoffed. "Don't be too gracious. I may change my mind."

She laughed with wild abandon and danced out of his grasp. "Something smells good. Other than the flowers, I mean."

Craig pulled her close for one more kiss and escorted her to the table, where he proceeded to serve dinner. He sat across from her. They said grace. Pat's phone rang.

"That's probably Melena."

He waited while she answered.

"Hey, girl. Yeah, I'm here. Got sidetracked. Some crazy man filled the house with flowers and food. We're about to eat now." She ended the call, apologized, and silenced the phone.

They talked through dinner and while washing the dishes. He told her how building the cabin was moving along, rather slowly, since he was basically a one-man construction company. Richard helped as much as he could after school. And the previous weekend, Ace, and Stanley, had pitched in. Since Mike was on call most of the time, he could not work as often as he'd like.

"Well, starting tomorrow, you'll have another pair of hands. If you'll have me."

The sensual undertone to her suggestion simmered in his blood. He caressed her palm with his fingers. "Oh, I'll have you all right. Wouldn't want to put callouses on these beautiful hands, though."

The quick flare that changed her eyes from smoky blue, to violet, assured him the innuendo wasn't lost on her.

"These hands are a lot stronger than you think." So, saying, she took one of his larger appendages in both of hers, kissed the palm, then pressed it against her cheek.

Craig slid his free hand around her waist, edged her closer, and captured her mouth in a deep, shuddering kiss. When she turned toward the bedroom, he hesitated. "I…"

She halted his protests with a finger over his mouth. "I want to lie with you, Craig. To hold, and be held by, you." A tiny smile tugged at that lovely mouth. A twinkle lit her gaze. "I promise not to tease or tempt you into more than you're ready to give."

He couldn't stop the laugh rumbling in his chest or the love bursting in his heart. "Sounds like something I should be telling you."

She giggled and led the way. Stopping long enough to remove their shoes, they crawled onto the mattress, and stretched out beside one another. Pat rested her head on his shoulder. "This is nice."

Craig draped an arm around her waist, caressed her back, and hummed in agreement.

Her hand journeyed across his chest and traced the seams of his shirt. He hesitated when she fingered the chain around his throat.

"May I?"

Craig swallowed hard and nodded. If he loved her an hour before, his sentiments doubled when she gasped and murmured, "How beautiful," while holding Tamera's cross, and his wedding ring, in her palm.

"The cross will go to Tamera Joy one day."

"And the ring?"

He shrugged. "My grandson, I guess."

"Where are Tamera's rings?"

"Lexie wears them." Tears filled his eyes, and rolled down his cheeks, as he recollected, aloud, how his daughter-in-law had looked, in his wife's wedding dress, the day she married his son.

She kissed the spot where his jewelry had lain. "The way your family is so close-knit is beautiful. Mel's is like that. They're the only family I have since my parents are gone."

Craig sat up, cradled her face in his hands, and covered her mouth in a gentle caress. "No matter where our relationship goes, you'll always have a place in mine. If you want it." The joy reflected in her expression would warm his heart forever.

Chapter Nineteen

Pat awoke shivering. Donning her robe, she found the thermostat, and turned on the furnace. Within moments, a toasty warmth permeated the cabin, enhancing the smell of roses. Her phone vibrated.

Melena asked via text message how things were going.

Just getting up. I'll call you later. She noticed a missed call from Craig and listened to his voicemail...

"I guess you forgot to turn the ringer back on. Unfortunately, your voice wasn't the last thing I heard before sleep or first thing this morning. Thank you for a wonderful evening. If you want to drive out to the cabin today, get there by..."

Pat listened to his detailed directions while she brewed a pot of coffee. Since the days were short, and she'd slept later than she ever had, in her entire life, she'd meditate tonight. Dressing, she headed out to meet him, calling Melena on the way.

"So...?"

Pat laughed. "Roses. Everywhere. Inside and out. He also brought dinner. His daughter had cooked a huge meal, and his daughter-in-law provided dessert. You know I'm not much on red meat, but the roast melted in my mouth. It was close to midnight when I took him to the Crossed Penn to retrieve his truck."

"How romantic! Why didn't he just spend the night?"

"He's... I don't know... There's something about him... An old-fashioned sense of chivalry and respect... Loyalty and honor I've never experienced with another man. Except for Scott. He wears his wedding ring on a chain around his neck with a cross his wife gave him on their wedding day."

"Yeah. I wore mine like that too."

They lost signal. Pat disconnected her end of the call and pondered what she'd told Melena. How much Craig resembled the man she remembered Scott to be, continued to astound her. Most men wouldn't have hesitated to jump into bed with her. Or initiate the same result.

Promiscuous by no means, she'd never bought into the archaic idea that a man and woman who cared deeply for one another would go to hell for expressing those feelings on the physical level. Nor did she believe an exclusive, committed, long-term relationship equaled sexual immorality.

Pat knew her views on the matter irritated people in both of the "premarital sex" camps. She usually didn't care about what folks would say. She *did*, however, care what Craig thought. How he felt. What his children might think. Either way, she'd respect and honor him as much as he did her.

She'd wait for his lead into the next phase of their relationship.

She arrived at the gate of the Rockin' H, punched in the code, and waited for it to swing open. *A whole lot easier than the previous trip.* She followed the path to the cabin, well-worn from constant usage the last few weeks, where she found Ace, Stanley, and Craig, hard at work. Cutting. Hammering. Framing.

She parked her car alongside their vehicles, exited and walked to where they stood, discussing what to do next. "Hey guys, how can I help?"

Craig's son and son-in-law tipped their hats, and simultaneously, bid her good morning. He lifted her off her feet in a bear hug. A far cry from the last time she was here.

"The four of us should be able to get those walls up now." Craig consulted his watch. "And Richard will be here soon. Going to be a productive day, boys. Let's get to work."

They paired up and got busy.

Richard arrived around one o'clock, along with Amber, and Lexie, who'd brought everyone water, coffee, and snacks. Pat found herself clasped in a firm embrace. "Shame on you, Daddy, for putting her to work."

"I volunteered. You must be Lexie." Pat extended a hand toward the auburn haired, green-eyed beauty.

"So nice to meet you, Ms. Pat. You should come back to the house with us and let these yahoos do whatever it is men do."

Pat didn't miss the light in either of the younger women's eyes when they looked at their 'yahoos.' She grinned. "I'm used to working around men. Mostly doctors with God complexes."

Lexie and Amber hooted. "Can't be any worse than cowboys with 'em."

"Hey, no male bashing," the guys yelled in unison, instigating a bout of teasing and jostling.

Craig whistled. "All right, either grab a hammer or go away. We're burning daylight."

The love in his expression belied the severity of his words. Pat edged closer to him and whispered, "Should I be afraid?"

He chortled. "Very."

She knew he was teasing and rolled her eyes, then followed the girls back to the ranch house where she met Katrina and Little Ace, who stole her heart with how much he resembled his father and grandfather. The moment her hands clasped those of Scott's widow, their eyes met. Souls connected.

Over the next couple of hours, they shared stories of how each met Scott. She laughed with her, when Trina told of meeting him on the highway, after she and her first husband were involved in a single-car accident. And, how stubborn and over-protective he'd been from the start.

Her heart sighed with the romance of it all when Katrina regaled her with accounts of their wedding and near-perfect marriage. And how Lexie had been brought into their lives. "He must have made quite an impression for you to remember him so vividly after more than thirty years."

Pat nodded. "He was one of a kind. Or so I thought." She locked gazes with Amber. "Until I met Craig."

"Yeah. No doubt they're cut from the same cloth."

Pat took Trina's hands in hers. "I don't know what he told you about his first wife, and I don't really want to get into all that. But I am *so* glad he met you and found happiness after so many years of the opposite and such a tragic ending."

Trina smiled. "Only the barest details. Thank you, though."

Mike arrived around four o'clock in an SUV loaded with kids. One by one, Pat met Craig's granddaughters, oldest grandson, and Trina's other two children. Mike must have sensed her near overwhelm, because he laughed, and assured her, there wouldn't be a test on who was who, and belonged to whom.

"Whew. Good thing."

He settled at the table while Amber, Lexie, and Trina, hustled their children into various rooms with snacks and homework. "I saw Missy today."

"Really?"

"Yeah. Turns out she's one of my patients."

"Good. I haven't had a chance to run out and check on her. She's OK?"

He nodded. "She's fine."

Pat noticed how his countenance lit up when Trina returned.

"Get 'em settled for now?" he asked.

Neither did Pat miss the smile Trina bestowed on him, when she answered affirmatively, and poured him a cup of coffee.

Shortly after dark, the men came in from work, causing a flurry of activity. Kids ran in to greet their father, grandfather, or uncle. Mild chaos ensued over what they'd have for dinner. When the votes for pizza outweighed those against it, Craig told his daughter to call in the orders.

"I'll clean up a bit, then we'll get them." He turned to Pat. "You are staying, right?"

Her reasons for going home were drowned out by a loud chorus of pleas for her to stay.

Ashlyn, one of Craig's twin granddaughters, approached them. "Can I ride with you to get the pizza, PaPaw?"

Pat nodded when he arched a questioning brow at

her.

"Sure. If it's OK with your parents."

"Mom, I'm riding with PaPaw to get the pizza!"

"That didn't sound like you were asking for permission."

The gentle rebuke in Craig's tone caused a flush to fill the teen's cheeks. He ran upstairs to freshen up. Pat sensed a deeper reason why the girl wanted to ride with them. She went over to where Ashlyn talked with her parents about tagging along. "Would you like some private time with your grandfather, sweetheart?"

Ashlyn raised shy, sapphire eyes to hers, and nodded.

Pat smoothed a hand down her arm. "You go with him, then."

Craig bounded down the stairs. "Y'all ready?"

The girl's smile could have melted the hardest of hearts.

Pat walked with them to the door. "You two go. I'll wait with the others. We'll talk later," she insisted with a meaningful look when Craig started to balk.

He caressed her cheek with his knuckles and vowed to hurry.

"That was kind of you," Amber said, stepping into the foyer.

Pat shrugged. "I sensed she needed some time alone with him."

A worried frown creased Amber's brow. "She's always been his favorite. Although he's made sure none of the other kids knew. She's been a bit moody lately. Typical teenage angst, I guess."

"Then time with her PaPaw is the best thing for both

of them."

Amber slipped her arm through Pat's. "I've a feeling you'll be good for all of us."

Chapter Twenty

Craig waited until they were on the way into Bandera, to address his granddaughter. "Something on your mind, sweetheart?"

"Are you going to marry Ms. Pat?"

Not knowing yet what was bothering her, Craig chose his words carefully. "A little soon for us to be talking marriage. But if we were, would that bother you?"

"No. Guess I've just been missing MaMaw lately."

"You remember your grandmother?" She was barely more than two when Tamera died.

"Hard not to when I look exactly like her."

Craig reached out and squeezed her hand, raised it to his mouth, and kissed the back. "Yes. You do. But no one expects you to *be* her. What's really bothering you, Ash?"

The pain and confusion on her face tugged at his heart. "I don't know. Sometimes, I wish she hadn't died. That I got to know her better. And sometimes, I want to go meet her."

His heart plunged into his stomach. "Our loved ones are never really gone, sweetheart. Their spirit lives on, in our hearts, and our memories. Any of us can address everything you want to know about her, baby. But going to meet her before it's time is not really an option. Now is it?"

"Guess not. I just don't fit in anywhere."

"What gives you that idea?"

"Kids at school. Even Kaitlyn doesn't understand me, and we're supposed to be best friends."

"Everyone goes through growing pains, Ash. You

and Kaitlyn will always be sisters, no matter who your best friends are."

Her sigh echoed through the truck and spoke volumes. "Your mama had similar problems in high school."

"Really?"

Craig nodded. "Yeah. But she never let what others thought define who she was. What she did. Or what she believed. You'd be wise to do the same. You're a beautiful, smart, sensitive young lady, and I'm so proud of the way you're growing up."

He pulled into the pizzeria's lot, parked the truck, unbuckled, and got out then walked around to open her door. The moment she slid into his arms Craig held on tight. "Promise me, Ashlyn, that you'll talk to someone when you feel lost or left out. Me, your mom, or dad. Trina, or Lexie. We've all felt this way from time to time. It's normal, and I can assure you, you will get through it. Ms. Pat would even be a good person to talk to."

Ashlyn beamed. "I like Ms. Pat. A lot."

"So do I."

They retrieved the food and continued talking all the way back to the ranch.

After dinner, when everyone started getting ready to take their family home, Craig walked with Pat to her car. "I wish you'd stay here tonight. I hate to think of you on the road, alone, so late."

"Where, and in what, would I sleep?"

He hummed. "Interesting dilemma. I'm sure we can come up with a solution."

Her good-natured laugh filled his heart with joy. "Not going to happen, Cowboy. Not here, with a house full of people."

His suggestions on solving the issue of sleepwear and arrangements–she could stay at the B&B. Amber or Trina would have something for her to wear. They could wash her clothes–were all met with staunch insistence that she'd be fine. Remembering Tamera's warning not to be too overprotective, Craig let her go with a kiss and an assurance that she'd call him the moment she reached Garrett's cabin.

He bid his daughter's family and Mike, Trina, and her brood goodbye, then went upstairs to shower and get ready for bed. Donning flannel pajama pants, a long-sleeved thermal undershirt, and thick socks, he waited for Ace on the porch. And laughed when his son settled in the chair beside him with a longsuffering sigh. "You sound about as old as I feel."

Ace chuckled. "Funny how soft we get when we don't tax our muscles regularly like we did today."

"Yeah. But we got a lot done. I appreciate you, and Stanley, pitching in when you can. Richard is a great help, but six pairs of hands is always better than two."

"Ms. Pat sure pulled her weight today."

Craig nodded. "Yes, she did."

"You really like her, don't you, Dad?"

"Yes, Ace. I do. As I said to Stanley, I hadn't felt a spark of, anything, with any woman, since your mother died. Until I met her. Not that some hadn't tried to rouse my interests the few times I ventured out by myself. And, as I told Mike, I'm not sure if it's her or simply me coming into it on my own, but I'm not going to ignore the rare and precious gift of her friendship."

"Well, everyone seems to adore her. She sure made

an impression on Amber when she declined riding with you to get supper so that Ashlyn could spend some time alone with you. How is she, by the way?"

Craig sipped his drink. "Ashlyn is going through some emotional turmoil with kids at school. We all need to watch her a bit closer. Make concerted efforts to show her how loved and valued she is."

"She looks more like Mama every day."

"That she does." Craig's phone rang, stopping further conversation. Ace went inside so he could talk in private. "Hello?"

"Made it home safely, Cowboy. I'll see you tomorrow."

"Good deal. Sweet dreams."

* * *

Thus began their routine for the next couple of weeks. When not helping at the Crossed Penn, Pat lent a hand in building the cabin. Weekends were filled with familial bonding along with the work. The promise of bonfires and s'mores provided incentive for the younger kids to haul boards, hand out nails or other materials, and pick up trash.

Many times, Pat escaped hard labor by aiding Amber, Katrina, or Lexie in preparing meals, which were consumed on makeshift tables at the jobsite. A couple of times, she and Craig slipped off for an afternoon or evening alone. Dinner. Dancing. A movie. Horseback riding. Before either of them realized the passing of time, the day came for him to drive her to the airport.

Craig parked at the terminal, got her luggage out of

the truck, and then opened her door. "I wish you were staying here, or I was going with you."

Pat hugged him. "Me too, Cowboy. Enjoy Christmas with your family. I'll be back before you know it."

His goodbye kiss left her trembling with need. She stayed on the curb and waved until he was out of sight, then checked in, and waited for her flight. Melena picked her up in Baton Rouge. They spent the night in a hotel, swapping stories, and giggling like school girls.

The following morning, Melena drove Pat to her home in Magnolia, where Garrett met them and handed her the keys to his truck. "Now you can get around, to the various parties, and not be on foot, or dependent on someone for a ride."

Pat thanked him with a hug and called Craig the minute she was alone.

"So, when will you be back?"

"I just got here."

"And your point might be...?"

Pat laughed. "We were originally supposed to head back the day after Christmas. But since Melena's kids– Jon and Kathryn–used their vacation time to go to the wedding, they're not able to take the extra time off work to go back to the ranch like they normally do. So, we'll be leaving shortly after the first."

"Awe, I wanted to ring in the New Year with you."

"Me too. But it is what it is."

"Maybe I could drive over and bring you back."

"That'll put a dent in the progress you're making on the cabin."

"I'll make it up later. Hire additional help if I have to."

"Guess I'll see you a couple of days after Christmas."

Chapter Twenty-One

Craig hung up with Pat and called the auto mechanic shop to schedule an appointment to have his truck serviced two days after Christmas. He only had a couple of days to work before the holiday festivities began and was blessed to have Richard, Robert, Ace, and Stan's help. Even his teenaged granddaughters pitched in, allowing him to make significant headway toward completing the structure's exterior design.

When everyone gathered on Christmas Eve, Craig realized the hole in his heart was not as empty as it had been in years past, but full of gratitude, joy, and promise. Long after everyone parted for the night, and Ace's family settled down to wait for good old Saint Nick, he and Pat talked, sharing laughter at the antics of the youngest children on both sides of their respective families. They did the same on Christmas day. He spent the twenty-sixth, alone, doing what he could at the cabin.

The following morning, after the mechanic deemed his truck "road trip ready," Craig settled in for the long drive to Mississippi. Memories filled his mind of the many times he'd traversed these same roads, to visit Scott's family in Lafayette, or while on their way to Tamera's childhood home. Magnolia wasn't as far as Greenville, but he stayed the night in a hotel in Louisiana anyway. No sense in having Pat wait up for him to drive straight through. Especially since he hadn't departed until after ten.

He arrived at the address she'd given him shortly before noon on the twenty-eighth, pleased to find her all alone. Waiting for him with open arms.

"You made it!"

Craig laughed. "Did you doubt I would?"

Desperate for the taste of her, he buried his hands in her hair and captured her lips in a passionate embrace. They spent the rest of the day, wrapped in a blanket on the porch swing, and cuddled together for the remainder of the night. Craig awoke the next morning alone, and fully clothed, except for his shirt and boots. He remembered falling asleep with her in his arms but had no recollection of her getting out of bed.

"Pat?" He tumbled from beneath the covers and walked toward the kitchen, passing a closed door on the way with a sign that said, *Quiet, Please, Meditation/Yoga in progress.*

Craig decided to take a shower and retrieved his duffle bag from the truck and. When she still hadn't emerged from her room, he decided to find the nearest donut shop and florist. He turned the coffee pot on and wrote a note saying he'd be back in a bit.

He returned with a dozen roses and just as many mixed-flavored donuts. She accepted the flowers with a smile but frowned at the box of sweet confections under his arm. "We'll have to talk about your eating habits, Cowboy."

Craig chortled. "There's an unwritten rule that eating habits go out the window when you're traveling." He put the box down, took her in his arms and kissed her. "Good morning, beautiful."

She smiled, and his heart skipped a thud. He poured coffee while she put paper plates, and napkins, on the table. Sitting, each reached into the box, bit into their pastry of choice, and hummed in unison. Which set off a peal of laughter.

Pat licked lemon filling off her fingers. His gut tightened at the innocent gesture. He leaned forward and removed some of the same from the corner of her mouth with his tongue. Her sharp intake of breath shivered through him like a caress. She cleared her throat and tilted back in her chair. "We're going to Melena's for dinner. She and Garrett are excited to meet you."

"Sounds good. What're we going to do until then?"

"Thought I'd show you around town. Let you see where I grew up. Do a little more sightseeing after lunch and on the way to Melena's."

"I thought she lived here."

Pat shook her head. "Not any more. Sold the house she and Jon lived in and bought a cottage a couple of hours north of here."

"OK. I'm ready when you are."

The next few days passed in a flurry of activity. Craig enjoyed every minute with Melena and Garrett. Surrounded by her children and grandchildren was as chaotically fun as having his all around. They had finished cleaning up after lunch on New Year's Day, and debated whether to drive straight through to Bandera, or split the trip into two days, when Pat received a phone call that changed everything.

Something in the jangle of her ringtone grated on Craig's nerves and set his teeth on edge.

"Hey, Doug. What's up?"

Pat walked away from the group as Melena whispered, "Her boss," in response to Craig's question of who Doug was.

"*What?* Oh, my God!"

The three of them rushed into the living room as Pat's knees buckled and her butt hit the floor. Her entire body shook with sobs. "Yeah... I'm here. I'll be there. No worries."

She disconnected the call and stared at them in shock. "I... Doug's..."

Craig lifted her to her feet. Melena rubbed her back. Garrett got her a glass of water. Pat's hand trembled as she drank, spilling droplets of liquid onto her sweater. She batted at them and visibly struggled for control.

"What is it, honey?" Melena asked.

"I..." She swallowed hard. "I've got to go to Rio de Janeiro. Doug's been called to treat a dozen or so children who were rescued from a child trafficking ring. He needs my help."

Every ounce of blood in his body drained from Craig's limbs. He shook his head and opened his mouth to protest, but only, "No," came out in a harsh whisper.

Pat's head jerked up. Eyes narrowed. She drew herself to her full five-feet-three-inches, and went nose to nose with him, her words punctuated by sharp jabs in his chest with her fingertip. "Don't tell me what I can and can't do. It's my job."

"It's too dangerous." The words spewed through teeth clenched as tightly as the fists by his side. Craig stumbled back from her assault. His eyesight blurred into tunnel vision, where all he saw was her boarding a plane to a foreign land, and not coming back. He snapped out of it in a wave of fear and fury. "You can't. I won't lose you too!"

"You're asking me to give up what I love!"

Craig spun on his heel and stormed out of the house.

The door slammed in his wake. His breath heaved in and out of his chest in jagged pants. He whirled on him when Garrett placed a hand on his shoulder. "I…"

Garrett stopped further comments with a shake of his head. "The hardest thing about starting over, is letting go of the fears that have held you back."

Craig nodded and swallowed the hard knot of bile burning his throat.

* * *

Pat started after him. Melena grabbed her by the arm to stop her. "Give him a moment, Pat. Garrett's gone after him."

She yanked free. "Mel…"

Melena took her by both shoulders and gave a little shake. "Don't you dare 'Mel' me. I won't let you go out there and say something you'll regret later."

"No man is going to dictate ultimatums to me."

"He didn't do that. He simply expressed his fears. Pull yourself together and give him a minute to do the same."

"I don't have a minute. Doug's bought my ticket on the redeye out of Baton Rouge. I've got to get to the airport."

"OK. Let's go get your things."

Melena escorted her through the garage door out back and drove them to Pat's house. Pat had barely finished packing her suitcase when Craig arrived.

He went into the bedroom where he'd slept the last few nights and threw his things into his duffle bag, stopping beside them on the way out. "I'll take her."

"Pat?" The fear and concern on Melena's face neutralized her anger. Pat agreed with a slight incline of her chin.

Melena hugged her. "OK. Be careful and please, *please* call me as often as you can. I'll see you when you return.

She turned to Craig. "Meeting you has been a real pleasure. Garrett, and I, will contact you when we get to Utopia."

Craig thanked her, rattled off his cellphone number, then picked up Pat's suitcase and put it in the truck along with his bag. A tense, wary silence clouded the atmosphere the entire hour and a half it took to get from Magnolia, Mississippi, to the airport in Baton Rouge.

Already regretting her harsh response to his fear had Pat's feelings in an uproar. Never in her life had she reacted out of such blatant emotion as she had since meeting Craig. She struggled with what to say. How to say it. Whether or not she should reach out to him. Before she could calm the crazy whirlwind of her thoughts, he pulled up to the terminal gate. Pat waited while he disembarked, and walked around to open her door, before unbuckling her seatbelt, and climbing down from the cab.

He cupped her face in his hands. "Let me make this clear. I am not asking you to give up what you love. I am asking you to consider other options."

The dam burst. Pat found herself enveloped in a crushing hug. The initial boarding call for her flight came across the intercom. She pressed her lips to his cheek and whispered, "I'll see you when I get back, Cowboy." She grabbed her suitcase and hurried through the doors.

Chapter Twenty-Two

Craig couldn't get out of Baton Rouge quick enough. He found his way to Interstate 10 and pointed the truck westward, determined to drive as far as possible tonight. A flat tire, and two speeding tickets later, he second-guessed his decision. He figured he'd call it a night when lights flashed in his rearview mirror for the third time. He eased onto the side of the road, and rolled down the window, as the state trooper approached.

"Driver's license and registration, please."

Craig handed over the requested items. Dread filled his heart at the expression on the officer's face when he walked toward him once more.

He looked at the notes in his hand, then at Craig. "Forget how to use your cruise control, buddy?"

"No, sir."

A penlight flashed in his eyes.

"You been drinking?"

Craig shook his head. "Not yet." *But he was damn well going to.*

"I think you need to shut it down. Hotel or jail cell?"

"Hotel."

"Follow me. Don't get lost."

"Yes, sir."

He didn't have to wander far from his room to the hotel bar for that first stiff drink. The following morning, he woke up with a headache from hell. Putting one cautious foot in front of the other, he made his way into the shower and washed away most of the dregs from last night's foray into alcoholic bliss. He dried off and dressed. Using the towel, he wiped the fog off the bathroom mirror, taking in the pale complexion, and pain reflected in his bloodshot eyes. *Bliss, my ass.* He curled a fist in the towel to keep from putting it in the glass.

Oh, God. What have I done? What am I going to do? Temper...

He felt her presence. Heard her voice urging him to hang on. To not give up. On life. On love. On second chances.

Craig finished his morning grooming, and took advantage of the breakfast bar, before continuing his journey home. He stopped at the cemetery to visit his wife and then went out to the cabin. Not wanting to face his children yet, he had dinner in town, and meandered about until after midnight.

The following morning, and many after, he was up and gone before the first patter of younger feet hit the floor.

* * *

Pat retrieved her suitcase from baggage claim and looked for the driver Doug was supposed to have sent. She was scrolling through her messages when the phone rang. Mike Guidry. Her heart lurched. "Hey, Mike. Everything OK?"

"Yep. Hey, you wouldn't be interested in working with me, would you? I'm getting pretty busy, and a nurse practitioner might be more feasible than bringing in another doctor."

The instant flare of anger obliterated all reasonable thoughts from her brain. She ground her teeth so hard it's a wonder she didn't spit dust when she opened her mouth. After all these hours berating herself for her lack of sensitivity! "Did Craig put you up to this?"

"N...no... I haven't talked to Craig since Christmas. He's not with you?"

The spurt of fear she experienced seeing his name on her phone, burst within her breast, at the thought of something happening to Craig. "No. He's not with me. I'm at the airport in Rio de Janeiro. Craig should be back in Bandera by now."

Mike must have heard the thread of panic in her voice because he rushed to reassure her. "Just because I haven't seen him, doesn't mean he's not back. What are you doing there?"

Pat explained her mission and then disconnected the call before she had a total meltdown. She spent the remainder of her trip to the encampment where Doug and the children were, pleading with God that Craig was safe, and she'd hear from him soon.

Two days later, Pat realized she'd have to be the one to take the first step in breaching the chasm between them. After all, she'd overreacted as much as he. She knew Tamera's death had been brutal for him, and that he was only beginning to find his way back to life. Partly thanks to her. She'd text him soon. The first order of business was a conversation with Doug. *More like confrontation.*

Either way, she had to do what she had to do.

Printing out her resignation on the office machine, she brooked no argument when she gave it to him. "You've got two weeks to get someone out here to replace me. Either way, I'm done and outta here. My heart, my *spirit,* can't take this anymore."

He argued. Pleaded. Whined. But Pat stood her ground, and in the end, he wished her luck in whatever she decided to do with her life.

Strolling back to her barracks on proverbial cloud nine, Pat took the next step in reconciling her dreams and desires with the love in her heart. Offering forgiveness had always come easier than asking for it, but she took the chance. She sent Craig a text message apologizing, asking forgiveness, expressing her love, and waited two days for his answer.

"Come home. Safe. And soon," was all she heard before they lost the connection.

* * *

Three weeks later, her return to Bandera was both a celebration and a reunion. Craig had hired a construction firm and completed most of the work on the cabin. The rest they'd do together.

His entire family, along with Garrett, and Melena, gathered around a table laden with food as they wrapped up removing debris from the area. You could have heard an ant crossing the grass when Craig took both of her hands in his and cleared his throat loud enough to bring everyone to complete silence. "Pat..."

Her heart began to thrum. "Yes?"

"If there's one truth I've learned in all of my years on this earth, it's that life is a journey. One of highs and lows and winding roads. Blessed with joy. Tempered by heartache. Filled with broken dreams which can be fired up again with new hope. New passion. I want to travel the rest of mine with you." He took a ring out of his shirt pocket. "Will you marry me?"

Cheers rent the evening sky when she threw herself in his arms with a squeal. "Yes!"

Mike slipped his arms around Katrina's waist and pulled her close. "Dang, I couldn't have said that better myself."

She laughed. "You call that a proposal, Dr. Guidry?"

He dropped to one knee and held out a box. "No. But this is. Katrina Hensley, will you do me the honor of becoming my wife?"

Once more, cheers filled the air when she too, said yes.

Epilogue

On a beautiful day in late spring, the Harris/Hensley clan, along with Melena's family, and the Crossed Penn crew, gathered at the Hensley House B&B, to celebrate the impending nuptials.

The couples had decided on a double wedding.

After weeks of coaxing, Pat crawled out of her comfort zone enough to wear a solid dress that picked up the muted hues in Trina's floral-print wedding gown. Spared the discomfort of wearing tuxedos, Craig, and Mike, sported similar suits and ties. The two men stood in the courtyard awaiting their brides, when Mike noticed the pained expression on Lexie's face. "Oh, boy, hope we make it through the ceremony without interruptions."

"What do you mean?"

"A full moon has been known to induce labor and she is so close to delivering."

They walked to where she sat.

Mike squatted beside her. "Are you OK, sweetheart?"

Lexie tried to smile, grimaced instead. "My back hurts something fierce."

A low growl sounded in Ace's throat. "I tried to get her to stay home, but you know how stubborn she can be."

Mike shot Ace a look that commanded silence but the fear and worry on the younger man's face stopped him from commenting. He stroked Lexie's cheek. "No contractions?"

She shook her head. "A twinge here and there."

"What kind of twinges? Describe them."

She ran a hand over her abdomen. "Just tightness. Probably Braxton-Hicks."

Mike smiled and agreed. "You want to go inside and lie down a bit?"

"No, I'll be fine."

"Let's get you into a more comfortable chair." Motioning for Craig to follow, they moved a chaise lounge from the patio, and helped her into it. "Ask Trina for a small pillow to put behind her back and another for beneath her knees. We'll stay with her until you get back."

Ace nodded and went inside.

Once they had her settled, Mike crouched down, placed a hand on Lexie's belly, and allowed all the joy and excitement in his heart to shine through. "I'm about to marry the love of my life, Lex. Let me get that done, will you please?"

Her whole being relaxed. She giggled and drew him in for a hug. "We'll do our best."

He, and Craig, returned to the JP's side as everyone else took a seat in anticipation of the brides' entrance.

One-by-one, Craig, and Pat, as well as Mike, and Trina, vowed to love, honor, and cherish their respective spouses in a short, sweet, traditional, ceremony.

Later, while taking family pictures, Lexie hissed in a breath, and doubled over, as her water broke.

Considering she'd been uncomfortable all day, Mike assessed the situation quickly. "Get her inside, Ace. Craig, bring the SUV around."

His composure brought calm to the situation before chaos could ensue. He accompanied the expectant parents, stripping off his jacket, and rolling up his sleeves. Pat and Trina followed. "We're going to check and see where you are, sweetheart, then get you to the hospital. When did the contractions get worse?"

Lexie grabbed her abdomen as another rush of pain squeezed her middle. "About an hour ago. I think," she gritted through clenched teeth. "Oh!"

"Talk to me, Lex."

"Something's not right. I don't think we'll make it to the hospital. It's happening too fast. Please don't let anything happen to my baby!"

"Not on your life, sweetheart. Breathe, Lexie. My bag's upstairs," he told Trina, who hurried to get it.

"Maybe we should just get in the car and go."

Mike sought Ace's gaze, willing him to stay calm. "If that's what you want."

As he and Ace maneuvered her toward the vehicle, another contraction hit her hard, and more fluid puddled at her feet. She swooned. Ace swore, picked her up, and carried her into the nearest bedroom.

Even though she was like a daughter to him, years of experience made it easy for Mike to shield himself from the fear and panic swirling all around. "Pat, call an ambulance. Trina, we need towels or old bedsheets."

Mike scrubbed his hands and arms in the kitchen sink, tugged on gloves, and went into the room where Ace and Pat had helped Lexie into bed. He checked for dilation. "Yep, we're fixing to have a baby."

Ace and Trina held Lexie's hands and coached her breathing. Minutes later, Pat placed a squalling, squirming boy in Ace's arms. At Mike's surprised exclamation of seeing another head, Pat moved to his side and helped deliver a little girl.

The ambulance arrived moments after the babies were born. "What are you going to name them?" a paramedic asked, as they transferred the mother, and newborns, onto a gurney.

"We decided on Morgan Jayne for a girl or Morgan Scott for a boy. Had no idea there were two," Ace answered, his voice reflecting awe and wonder.

"Better think of something quick, birth certificates will need to be filled out."

"I don't want them to have the same first name. Morgan and Morgan sound like something you'd see on a billboard. How about…" Ace hesitated then kissed Lexie's cheek. "How about Morgan Jayne and Michael Scott?"

Lexie's exhausted smile held nothing but joy. "I like that."

Mike chuckled. "I'm honored."

Cheers and applause greeted the family as they were wheeled out and placed into the ambulance.

The festivities continued until late in the evening, toasting the brides, grooms, and new babies.

Two weeks later, Missy and Brock called to announce the birth of their baby girl, Heather Rose.

The End

Thank You so much for purchasing this book! I hope you enjoyed reading **Tempered Journey** as much as I loved writing it. If so, please consider leaving a positive review and posting it at online retailers and websites where readers gather and/or your social media platforms.

If this is your first experience with the Tempered series, go back to the beginning with **Tempered Hearts,** and follow these beloved characters throughout the years, as love crosses the lines of age, and strengthens the bonds of friendship.

To find out more about Pat and Melena's story, check out **My Heart Weeps**.

Dear Reader,

One thing I've learned in my years as a widow is that our loved ones are near us all the time. They want us to be happy, to live, and to love again.

As Craig mentioned in his proposal to Pat, life is a journey filled with adventures. Some exciting. Others, not so much. But with grace and gratitude, the challenges we face can be opportunities to grow as spiritual beings having a human experience.

Until later, may God bless and keep you, and yours, in the palm of His loving hand!

Sincerely,
Pamela S Thibodeaux
"Inspirational with an Edge!" ™
http://pamelathibodeaux.com

About the Author

Pamela S. Thibodeaux grew up in the town of Iowa, Louisiana. She is the mother of four (two by blood and two by marriage) and a grandmother. A deeply committed Christian, Pamela firmly believes in God and His promises.

"God is very real to me, and I feel people today need and want to hear more of His truths wherever they can glean them. People are hungry for practical (and real) Christian values, not some 'holier-than-thou' dictates which are impossible to believe and difficult to live up to," Pamela says.

"I do my best to encourage readers to develop a personal relationship with God. The deepest desire of my heart is to glorify God and to get His message of faith, trust, and forgiveness to a hurting world."

Email Pamela at: pam@pamelathibodeaux.com
Visit her website: http://www.pamelathibodeaux.com

Sign up to receive *Pam's Newsletter* and get a FREE short story.

Also: be sure to follow Pam on Social Media: FaceBook, Twitter @psthib, Instagram, Pinterest, GoodReads, and BookBub.

Other Titles by Pamela S. Thibodeaux

<u>Tempered Hearts</u> (book 1 in Tempered series)

An innocent veterinarian. A jaded cowboy. Will they get burned under a Texas sun or find the heat that leads to happily ever after?

Craig Harris has sworn off relationships. He's been burned and betrayed too many times to count. But when he crosses paths with the hot-tempered veterinarian his grandfather hired for the summer will he let go of hurt and mistrust to find the true love he's always longed for?

Tamera Collins is in no mood to put up with an arrogant jerk cowboy even if he is her boss. Grieving too-recent losses leaves her wary of the strong attraction between her and Craig. Can she overcome heartache and shattered faith and open up to their blossoming love?

<u>Tempered Dreams</u> (book 2 in Tempered Series)

He took an oath to preserve life. Can he stick to it when the woman he loves is in jeopardy?

Dr. Scott Hensley (introduced in Tempered Hearts) has built a wall around his heart since the death of his wife and parents. Katrina Simmons is recovering from scars inflicted on her as a battered wife. Can dreams be renewed and faith strengthened? Can they find joy and peace in God's love and in love for one another?

<u>Tempered Fire</u> (book 3 in Tempered Series)

The daughter of a wealthy rancher...A nobody from nowhere with nothing...Will their love survive?

Amber Harris is a good girl on the brink of womanhood. Stanley Morrison is a young man at the start of his life. For each other, they have always felt the fireworks that two people in love should feel. But the questions about his past, his pride, and Amber's father might be the end of what could be a strong relationship. As the two try to protect their budding romance, some unlikely but powerful forces conspire to keep them apart. Will they survive the wishes of everyone around them with their relationship intact?

Tempered Joy (book 4 in Tempered series)

He's an 'all around' cowboy. She thinks rodeo cowboys have rocks for brains and a death wish for a soul.

All around rodeo cowboy and heir to the Rockin' H Ranch, Ace Harris is determined not to fall in love. He's only loved one woman in his life, his mother, and no one can even come close to filling her boots. Lexie Morgan thinks rodeo cowboys have rocks for brains and a death wish for a soul. A broken childhood and the death of her father and best friend leave her doubting and questioning God (despite her years of religious upbringing) and afraid of love. Can two young people who clash from the onset learn to trust in the healing power of God and find love and happiness amidst tragedy and grief?

Tempered Truth (book 5 in the Tempered Series)

Will the truth set them free, or will it destroy a lifelong friendship?

Fate declared them neighbors. Scandal insisted they were brothers. The fact that they looked enough alike to be twins only added fuel to the rumors flying about their parentage.

For fifty-plus years Craig Harris and Scott Hensley have enjoyed a bond nothing can sever.

Not the insinuations that they share the same father.

Not the years of strife and grief and heartache.

Not even death.

Will the truth set them free, or will it destroy the friendship that has lasted a lifetime?

Lori's Redemption

Can a notorious bad girl find redemption & win the cowboy preacher's heart?

Lori Strickland (introduced in *Tempered Fire*) has always been known as her father's "wild child" with no desire to change until she meets ex-bull-rider-turned-preacher, Rafe Judson. Her attempts to change her wanton ways come to naught until she realizes redemption only comes with true repentance. Can she find redemption and win the heart of the cowboy preacher?

My Heart Weeps

When life takes everything, your world stops. Can a retreat heal the broken lives of two wounded souls?

Melena Rhyker's world shattered the day her husband died. Lost without the man of her dreams, she digs deep to find a path out of her sorrow. Discovering an artistic retreat, she vows to find a reason to carry on and focus her life in a new direction. Can she heal her own heart, and find her new beginning?

Garrett Saunders knows pain. He's spent most of his life hiding from his past. Regrets and lies haunt him, but he longs to leave them behind and embrace his true self. Will Melena's efforts to rebuild her life in the face of such grief encourage him to exorcise his own demons of guilt and shame?

Will two hurting people find peace, wholeness and perhaps love in the heart of Texas?

Get this second chance women's fiction novel today and see how love and faith conquers all.

Kyleigh's Cowboy

She's attempting to start a new life. He's roamed for more than a decade. Can they let go of the past and grab hold of the future?

Seven years after the death of her husband, Kyleigh Winters turned their old vacation home into a brand new guest ranch. Not willing to join the ranks of lonely women trolling the bars or online in search of a man, Kyleigh is sure if God wishes her to have another husband, He'll send the perfect someone in His own time. But will she be open to the possibility of new love when He does?

Searching for a place that calls to his soul, Lance Stevens has been a roaming cowboy for ten years since retiring from the Marines. He finds that sanctuary the moment he drives through the Silver Star's gate and meeting the lovely owner speaks to more than his soul. Will he open to the healing power of love?

Get Pamela Thibodeaux's second chance romance novella today and see how love and faith conquers all.

Keri's Christmas Wish

Controversy and Inconsistencies are thieves of holiday joy for Keri...is there any hope for a happy holiday season?

For as long as she can remember, Keri Jackson has despised the hype and commercialism around Christmas—especially with the controversy over the time of Jesus' birth. Will she get her wish and be free of the angst to truly enjoy Christmas this year?

Jeremy Hinton thinks Keri is a highly intelligent, deeply emotional, and intensely complex woman and he's as fascinated by her aversion to Christmas as he is of the woman herself. A devout Christian at heart, he's studied all of the world's religions and homeopathic healing modalities. But when a rare bacterial infection threatens her life, will all of his faith and training be for naught?

Fans of near death experiences will enjoy this woman's mystical journey into spiritual Truth.

Circles of Fate

When two souls are torn apart by duty, can the hand of God bring them back to a happily ever after?

Late Vietnam War era. Strapped for cash, Todd Jameson flirts with disaster. Caught robbing a liquor store to pay for his dad's funeral and given the choice of jail or signing up for the military, he picks the best of two bad options and joins the army. But just as his fresh start reconnects him with a sense of honor and the friendship of a gracious woman, he's deployed overseas into an unknown destiny.

Sixteen-year-old Shaunna Chatman devotes every

breath to caring for her sick mother. Working in a diner to make ends meet, the last thing on her agenda is to fall for a young soldier about to be sent into battle. But when he encourages her not to wait, she reluctantly moves on to wed another who's there to pick up the pieces after she buries her beloved mom.

Thrown into a whirlwind of circumstance, Todd flows in and out of the courageous girl's narrative wondering if their stories will ever fully entwine. And though Shaunna's journey grants her a child even as personal tragedy strikes, her thoughts often turn to the boy who still fills her heart.

Will their paths merge once more to bask in the glory of His love?

Circles of Fate is a deeply woven inspirational women's fiction novel. If you like believable heroes, roads to enlightenment, and tales of inner strength, then you'll adore Pamela S Thibodeaux's romantic saga.

Buy *Circles of Fate* to walk in the light today!

The Visionary

Will the ugly secret haunting the twins keep them from finding true love?

While most visionaries see into the future, Taylor sees the past. but only as it pertains to her work. Hailed by her peers as "a visionary with an instinct for beauty and an eye for the unique" Taylor is undoubtedly a brilliant architect and gifted designer. But she and twin brother Trevor, share more than a successful business. The two share a childhood wrought with lies and deceit and the kind of abuse that's disturbingly prevalent in today's society.

Can the love of God and the awesome healing power of His grace and mercy free the twins from their past and open their hearts to the good plan and the future He has for their lives?

Love is a Rose *(devotional)*

Can God use a secular song to speak to someone and touch their heart?

Music is the magical entry into the spirit world, the golden gate into the Kingdom of God. But we mustn't be of the mindset that God only uses Christian music to reach out and touch our mind, heart, and spirit. God uses any and ***every*** means available to speak to His children.

Our job is to be open and receptive.

In this devotional, Pamela S Thibodeaux shares how God opened her spirit to a deeper understanding of the abundance of His grace and mercy through the words of the song, The Rose sung by Country & Western artist Conway Twitty.

Pamela offers Seeds to Ponder and a prayer as she parallels the love of God and the Christian life to each verse of the song.

Love's Overcoming Power eBook

Temptation, Abuse, Grief, and Doubt are plagues common to women all over the world. In John, 16 Jesus said.... In the world you will have tribulation but be of good cheer, for I have overcome the world.

In this Women's Fiction collection comprised of three full-length novels and one novella, Pamela S Thibodeaux shares stories that exemplify the power of

God's love to overcome whatever situations life throws at you.

Includes: ***The Visionary, Circles of Fate, My Heart Weeps*** and ***Keri's Christmas Wish.***

The Tempered Series Collection eBook

Start at the beginning and follow these beloved characters throughout the years as love crosses the lines of age and strengthens the bonds of friendship.

Contains: ***Tempered Hearts, Tempered Dreams, Tempered Fire, Tempered Joy, Lori's Redemption***

Praise for Pamela S. Thibodeaux

*"**Kyleigh's Cowboy** was so beautifully written, that it literally made me cry. The hero and heroine were sympathetic yet flawed and I fell instantly in love with them. Wonderful Christian Cowboy Romance!"* ~ Amazon Reviewer T.P. Warren

"Pamela Thibodeaux uses her masterful story writing art to create a powerful story of how God heals a woman's heart —broken by grief— through recovery, love and triumph." ~ CBA Best-Selling Author DiAnn Mills on **My Heart Weeps**.

"Loved this book. Wish everyone could read this. Definitely puts all holidays in perspective. If we remember the reason for the holidays then we must put God first........always. I will certainly recommend this book. Great stuff keep up the great writing." ~ (Amazon) Review of **Keri's Christmas Wish** by Reba

"Oh, the passion, faith and just LIFE that flows through this book...powerful writing indeed!" ~ Review of **Circles of Fate** by Deena Peterson, Book Reviewer @ A Peek at my Bookshelf and Just One More

"Thibodeaux leads the reader through from the first page to the last without once relinquishing control. She hooks them, holds them, and keeps them enthralled until the last line." ~ Review of **The Visionary** by Delia Latham, author of the "Solomon's Gate" series

*"If you have ever considered Christian fiction bland, then check out the **Tempered Series.** It will be well worth your time."* ~ Amanda Killgore for Huntress Reviews

*"**Lori's Redemption** is fast paced, lots of action, gripping storyline... I loved it. It's gone straight back into my TBR pile."* ~ Clare Revell author of the "Monday's Child" series

"Through Pamela's blessed ability to find God everywhere, even in secular song lyrics, she has written devotions guaranteed to touch the heart and remind the reader of our True Love, the Rose of Sharon." ~ Endorsement for **Love is a Rose** by Linda Yezak, Author, Editor Triple Edge Critique Service

Once Again, Thank You...

I pray you've been blessed as I have by your purchase of this book. If you've enjoyed ***Tempered Journey,*** please write a positive review, and post it at online retailers and websites where readers gather and/or your social media platforms (FaceBook, Good Reads, BookBub, Twitter, etc).

If you haven't already, sign up to receive my ***Newsletter*** and get a FREE short story.

**Temperance
Publishing**

www.ingramcontent.com/pod-product-compliance
Lightning Source LLC
Chambersburg PA
CBHW031156010826
48971CB00012B/746